...d
...n
Ancient Terrors
and Modern Insanities,
a Young Navajo
Searches for Truth

Spirit Warrior

DAVID GEORGE

REVIEW AND HERALD® PUBLISHING ASSOCIATION

Since 1861 | www.reviewandherald.com

Published by Review and Herald® Publishing Association, Hagerstown, MD 21741-1119

Review and Herald® titles may be purchased in bulk for educational, business, fund-raising, or sales promotional use. For information, e-mail SpecialMarkets@reviewandherald.com.

The Review and Herald® Publishing Association publishes biblically based materials for spiritual, physical, and mental growth and Christian discipleship.

The author assumes full responsibility for the accuracy of all facts and quotations as cited in this book.

Texts credited to NIV are from the *Holy Bible, New International Version*. Copyright © 1973, 1978, 1984, International Bible Society. Used by permission of Zondervan Bible Publishers.

This book was
Edited by Jeannette R. Johnson
Cover design by Trent Truman
Cover photo by PhotoDisc (*Note: Model on the cover is not the subject of the story.*)
Interior design by Candy Harvey
Electronic makeup by Shirley M. Bolivar
Typeset: Bembo 11/14

PRINTED IN U.S.A.

11 10 09 08 07   5 4 3 2 1

Library of Congress Cataloging-in-Publication Data

George, David Lane, 1958-   .
  Spirit warrior: suspended between ancient terrors and modern insanities, a young Navajo searches for truth / David Lane George.
    p. cm.
  ISBN 978-0-8280-1915-6
  1. Navajo Indians—Fiction. 2. Domestic fiction. 3. Christian fiction. I. Title.
PS3607.E64S65 2007
  813'.6--dc22

                           2006038770

Dedication

To the forgotten but precious Native people of North America . . .

especially the Navajo people,

who have taken me in as family and shared their life stories with me.

To order additional copies of *Spirit Warrior*, by David Lane George,
call 1-800-765-6955.

Visit us at **www.reviewandherald.com** for information
on other Review and Herald® products.

Acknowledgments

First, *to God*, for making me different and helping to make something useful and beautiful out of my life.

My wife, Lu, for sharing all my adventures in Navajoland, and for being the nearly "perfect" pastor's wife.

The children whom God entrusted to me:

> ***Benjamin,*** who pushed my car along a muddy Navajo trail more than once;

> ***Elannah,*** who brightens our home with her presence; and

> ***Yuel,*** for being a friend to so many needy children.

Grandma Vida Scholder, who pioneered Native work in New Mexico, and who showed me how to love it.

Mother Maude Fighting Bear, who gave me a Cheyenne name.

Monte Church, for his affirmations and encouragement.

Don Schneider, for giving me my first opportunity to serve in Native ministry.

Herman Bauman, for giving me my second opportunity to serve the Navajo people.

Robert Burnette, for helping me to grow spiritually and relationally.

Tricia (Positive Images in Missoula, Montana), for doing for this book what I could not do.

Darlene Knows His Gun, for being a good Navajo daughter.

My Assyrian dad, Ben, who still models faithful ministry for me.

My mom, Lila, whose gentle, indirect manners gave me a clue on how to communicate with Native Americans.

Aunt Linda, who always believed in me.

Papa Amos Russell, who adopted me into the Creek Nation and gave me wisdom and a name.

Shizhe'e Ike Beyale, who took me in and helped me learn about the ways of his people.

Shinai Tony Goldtooth and family, who helped me in countless ways.

The Nez and Tso families, who share their lives with me.

My Navajo sisters, Lorraine, Irene, and Elizabeth, for their loyalty.

The legendary pastor, Bud Joe Haycock, a true hero.

The Billy family, my joy and crown.

The Norton and Perry families, true missionaries to North America, and elsewhere.

Rachel and Randy Terwillegar, who gave from their hearts to the Native work.

Shirley Chipman, who continues to shine.

La Vida Mission, to whom I am deeply indebted.

Holbrook Indian School, for keeping their lights on.

Mamawi Atosketan Native School, for serving against all odds.

Bud, Linda, and the Trail of Hope.

The Cottonwood food bank.

Belkis Altamirano, a faithful typist.

Jeannette Busby Johnson, the Montana city girl who helped the story to be told.

My brother Dan . . . for being my brother!

Contents

CHAPTER 1 First Imprints 9

CHAPTER 2 Anglo Grace 15

CHAPTER 3 The Recurring Terror 19

CHAPTER 4 When Normal Is Strange 25

CHAPTER 5 A Journey Into the Pain 32

CHAPTER 6 The Widening Ditch 43

CHAPTER 7 Band-aids for the Soul 51

CHAPTER 8 Disillusioned Wanderings 62

CHAPTER 9 In Search of Good Medicine . . .74

CHAPTER 10 The Way to the Bottom 85

CHAPTER 11 Ditches by the Road of Light . .100

CHAPTER 12 The Cost of Greatness 112

YOU can make a difference! . .127

First Imprints

"My people are destroyed for lack of knowledge" (Hosea 4:6).

A SMALL THUNDER CLOUD GRUMBLED as it approached the mesa from the southwest. Among the cedars at the base of the mesa stood a young woman in a blue velvet blouse and broom skirt. Her long black hair fell below her silver concho belt as she arched her neck and squinted up at the sky. The tiny thunderhead was more a point of curiosity than a cause of concern, too small to be thundering. For a moment she wondered why.

Then, feeling a gentle tug on her skirt, she bent down with sudden amusement to her toddling nephew, Kee, and playfully scooped him up. Kee giggled with delight at the swing of her strong, slender arm. He liked looking into her dancing brown eyes, and gently plunked his soft forehead against her brow. She was his aunt Betty, who had held and nurtured him more than his own mother. There was something about his jet-black shock of hair and his chubby brown cheeks that she found completely irresistible.

Her free hand clutched some leftover table scraps, and she headed down toward the sheep pens, where she knew she would find the dogs. These creatures were not household pets. They were work partners, guardians, and the early warning system for both sheep and family. The young woman knew that the dogs would gladly welcome the leftover table scraps she clutched in her free hand.

As she approached the corrals a gentle rain began to fall. Again, she glanced up at the sky, surprised that any rain at all could be coming from such a small cloud. But in that parched country any rain is welcome and considered to be a good sign. She placed little Kee under the sheltering branches of a scrawny juniper tree and proceeded toward the dogs. They wagged their stubby tails at her approach, and in moments the scraps were gone. She felt a twinge of guilt for not being able to give them more, but for a family that was sometimes unable to provide enough food for its human members, this was simply another harsh fact of life.

Suddenly remembering her little nephew, she turned quickly to see how he was faring in the rain. Whatever momentary concern she may have felt was immediately relieved. He had found himself a worthy wrestling opponent in one of the juniper's limbs and was vigorously pressing it to the ground. Her tension released into delighted laughter as she walked toward him to gather him in her arms once again.

It was to be her last expression.

A sudden, blinding flash of brilliance and a deafening explosion brought it all to an end. Louder than a cannon, it echoed through the cracks in the rocks of the mesa above, and when it was gone, Kee's beloved Aunt Betty lay motionless among the rabbit bushes. The country-side returned to its peaceful state with no other sounds than the gentle rain and a small boy crying.

On the other side of a small hill not far away, one of the men of the family had just finished planting seeds and was returning to the camp when the lightning struck. The sound of the thunder surprised him but his steps didn't falter, because from childhood he had been taught to be brave. But in the silence that followed he heard the boy's cries and began to run. The scene that lay before him as he crested the brow of the hill would be for-ever etched into his memory: Betty lay on the ground, twitching, blood now trickling from her mouth. Little Kee, on his hands and knees, was crying and crawling toward her.

Other family members from two nearby hogans rushed outside and began to wail. *"Aadi, aadi!"* someone cried. The older man, already run-ning, accelerated his sprint and grabbed the toddler moments before he could reach out and touch his beloved aunt.

Lightning is one of the main elements of nature, and traditional Navajos believed it to be alive, one of the most powerful gods of nature.

The dead are also feared. The old ones say it is taboo to have anything to do with a dead body. It should not be touched, especially one that has been struck by lightning. Even trees that have been struck by lightning are to be avoided.

The man carried the crying little boy back to the other family members. He continued to struggle and cry, even when he was in his own mother's arms. He wanted to be back with his aunt Betty in the rabbit grass, and his little heart was hurt that he never reached her during those terrible moments.

The only person in the immediate family who would go near the place where Betty lay was the family elder. He alone possessed the needed ceremonial remedy, a ritual in which he offered a sacrificial offering of an ancient arrowhead to the lightning god. Even then, the elder would only move the body a few feet to the shallow grave that he had dug, and there he would bury Betty's remains and cover them with logs from the hogan.

The small child continued his cry for a long time, but by evening everyone in the old camp had carried their meager belongings to a location a hundred yards away and camped where they could see the shallow grave. It was not too close for the ghost of Aunt Betty to bother them, but it was close enough to guard the grave, day and night. They wanted to prevent any skinwalkers from extracting her body parts from the grave.

It was common knowledge that there were evil persons in their community who used dried human flesh—especially from one struck by lightning—to make evil potions that would hurt and kill other people. This was their way of using fear to gain power to control and manipulate the world around them. It was believed that after four days the soul of the dead would leave for the place of the departed, and anyone who had a knowledge of witchcraft or spiritism would no longer be able to invoke the spirit of the dead.

So having completed an uneventful four-day vigil, Kee's family moved farther away and set up a new camp on higher ground. In this way they hoped to begin a new life and put distance between them and the painful memory. But little Kee saw his mother and grandmother crying and wiping their eyes. Years later he would remember this moment. It was an imprint of pain and sorrow that he would struggle to overcome.

No one felt comfortable talking about it, and even when Kee was much older they would simply explain that the only way he would ever see Betty again would be in a dream, or if she came back as a ch'eendee (a ghost). This traditional teaching locked the unresolved grief in his heart and surrounded him with fear. Although he deeply missed his aunt and still loved her, he would be afraid to ever see her again. The event had been traumatic enough, but now the stage was being set for his long journey into addiction.

▼ ▼ ▼

Kee was strong—at least that's what Grandma said. She and his mother remembered the night before he was born, when a skinwalker had found them alone in their hogan. Even though that wintery night had been cold, he was naked except for a coyote's skin over his head. By day he was just another clothed, normal-appearing member of the community. But on certain evenings, as the sun began to set, he would answer an unspoken call, an inner urge for evil. It had happened many times before. In the fading light he would set out for the secret meeting place, usually a cave, where he would meet with others who, like himself, had sold their souls—and some of their family members—to the evil powers. In this exchange, the skinwalkers had received wealth, power, and sexual gratification. Many things were done in that cave that are too evil for one even to consider.

But now he was outside the hogan, chanting curses, and the two women heard his low, menacing voice mingling with the dogs' aggravated barking. Grandma cracked the door and peered into the darkness. The cold wind brought tears to the edges of her eyes that ran down her weathered cheeks. She saw the yapping dogs nervously shying away from a mysterious, hunched-over shape. Immediately she closed the door, bolted it, and gave her pregnant daughter a fearful look.

"There's something out there by the woodpile. It's bad!" She spoke with a soft intensity, her mind racing to consider her options. All the other relatives were gone, and she was miles from a phone. She sensed that showing their fear would only make it worse, and giving the skinwalker what he wanted was unthinkable.

"We must be strong," she said with a firmness her daughter understood. "We will sing the songs of the twin heroes." With that she broke into a high-pitched chant, soft and thin at first but gathering courage and volume as her daughter joined her. She thought about the twin Navajo heroes, who so long ago had ingeniously overcome great problems and challenges. They had received honor; and now, as their descendant, she claimed their heritage for herself, her daughter, and the unborn child as she sang. Their protection would be hers. It was both spiritual and physical. She pictured it. She believed it was hers.

Outside, the skinwalker crept closer, but the sound of the singing voices inside the hogan made him uncomfortable. He didn't like meeting resistance head-on. It was more effective when he could terrify his victims into submission. But he had chanted his curses, so now it was only a matter of time. He slunk away with sadistic pleasure at the thought of the pain that would someday come. A sudden snow began to fall and covered his tracks almost as quickly as he made them as he hurried back to the cave.

Whether it was the trauma of the evil visitor, the long night of singing, or just the right time is still uncertain. But before dawn, the young woman's labor contractions began. By the first light of morning they had intensified to the point that she had to tell her mother. The old woman knew the skinwalker would avoid the light of day, and so she made both of them ready for the long walk to Monument Valley Hospital. The thought of another night alone with a helpless mother and newborn was out of the question.

Once outside in the wintery weather, the laboring mother tired quickly. The snow had stopped falling, but it was deep enough to make each step increasingly difficult. The wind, too, had died down, but the icy temperature soon sapped their energy.

It was the older woman who was the strong one, breaking a trail through the snow until her daughter fell too far behind. Then she went back, and with her arm supported her daughter as they walked.

The contractions increased in their intensity until finally the young woman, despite her mother's help, doubled over and fell into the snow. "Get up! We're almost there!" coaxed her mother. "Look; there it is!"

It was true. Looking up, the younger woman saw the towering red stone formations all around her, and the hospital several hundred feet away. The snow sent a reviving rush up her arms and legs, but she was too tired to get up. So placing one hand in front of the other, she began to crawl on all fours. Once again her mother tried to get her to stand, but she crawled on, oblivious and resolute, until she had to pause for another contraction. When it subsided, she pressed on toward her impossible goal.

A woman, coming out of the small post office beside a row of trailers, saw her and ran to help. She and the old woman tried unsuccessfully to lift the mother-to-be from the snow, but she was dead weight, unable to do anything more than mechanically move toward the hospital, her brown limbs trembling. Finally they gave up and walked beside her, speaking encouragement. Somehow the freezing trio reached the hospital entrance, and the small staff jumped into action. They warmed the exhausted woman with hot compresses and somehow made it into the delivery room before Kee was born.

He was a long, slender baby, with a thick shock of black hair. That was why Grandma always said he was strong. In her mind this little grandson had proven that he was protected by a power that was able even to deflect the strike of a lightning bolt. It was a part of his heritage. So the skin-walker's curse on the night before Kee was born had eventually reached Aunt Betty instead.

This would not be the last curse that Kee would have to face.

CHAPTER 2

Anglo Grace

"How often I have longed to gather your children together, as a hen gathers her chicks under her wings" (Luke 13:34, NIV).

D R. MASON EXAMINED THE NEW MOTHER with his stethoscope, all the while aware of the watchful eye of Grandma, who was sitting in the corner of the hospital room. Something about his horn-rimmed glasses and short gray hair made her uneasy. It was said among her people that long hair was a sign of wisdom. Was this man foolish, or did the teaching only apply to Navajos?

Unlike some of her other relatives, Grandma never had anything bad to say about the Bilagaana (Anglo) people, even though less than 80 years before they had rounded up the Navajos and forced many of her ancestors on the "long walk," the Navajos' unique trail of tears. The memory of the cruel soldiers, under the leadership of Kit Carson, was still alive in the minds of the older ones. The soldiers had shot anyone who was too old, slow, or weak to keep up as the captives were marched to the New Mexico prison camp.

Grandma had been born on that grueling journey. Fortunately for Great-grandma, the baby had been born in the night, and her mother was strong enough to keep up the pace on the next morning's march.

Grandma was a little girl when the United States government granted the Navajos permission to return to their beloved land between the four sacred mountains. She remembered the going-home walk, a time of great happiness for her people.

Still the Bilagaana were not to be trusted.

The doctor had never seen either of the women before meeting them in the delivery room, but he was familiar with their timid nature toward strangers. He was long past being overly concerned about such things. He had already served for several years in this desolate place with its towering, red-sandstone crags, and had earned the respect of the Monument Valley community.

Sometimes he wondered what kept him here. Certainly not the scenery, though some of it was spectacular. No, he had only two reasons for being in this tiny Seventh-day Adventist hospital. One was his wife's great passion for these people, though it was a mystery even to him how deeply Alice loved "her" Navajos. Little else mattered—and her love was infectious! It seemed to transform its recipients, and they were many. There never seemed to be a shortage of Alice's love, despite the disappointments that came almost every day.

The miracle, in his mind, was how, after the long hours of work, they always managed to save something for each other. It was a fine line between hard work and burnout, yet they walked it frequently.

His other reason for staying was less dynamic but equally important: his own sense of duty and mission. He was part of a vanishing breed of medical professionals, who saw their training and skill not primarily as a money-making business but rather as a means of serving the needy of the world. He believed he was fulfilling his God-given task, and usually felt good about doing it.

Of course there were times in the middle of the night when a desperate pounding on the door would call him to stitch up a man who was bleeding from a knife fight, or to open his home to a fearful mother who needed shelter from an abusive husband. Sometimes those situations might tempt him to think about opening a practice in some quiet California community, but he never let himself think about it too long. He always reasoned that the "next life" would be his consolation.

He brought his attention back to his patient. "Well, I think you need to rest, but you are OK!" He said it, hoping that the new mother understood English.

She did, and mustered a faint smile in her dark eyes.

"My wife will come in pretty soon and pray with you," he said as he left the room.

It had been their standard practice for some time. They knew how much the Navajos—even those of the traditional religion—appreciated their prayers on such occasions.

And true to his word, later that afternoon the doctor's wife did arrive in the room. Her schedule had been altered somewhat when a physically abused woman came to her door. But she was used to that. The process of holding a woman as she cried, praying with her, and taking her some distance in her car to a hogan where her drunk husband would not be likely to find her hadn't diminished her glow. Her presence filled the room like a sunny spring morning, putting the two women at ease almost immediately. They looked with approval at her long silver hair that was pulled back in a pony tail. Her yellow blouse with its tiny red flowers was impressive, as well.

"Ya'at'eeh! I just saw your baby! He's beautiful!" she greeted them, following good Navajo manners by gently shaking their hands. "You must have had a long, hard walk coming here. It's cold out there!" She motioned to a sack in her left hand. "I made some sweet rolls this morning and thought you might be hungry. Supper won't be served for another two hours." She held out the bag to the new mother who gladly received it.

"I am wondering what you named him." She paused, knowing that these people were careful about giving out their names. "Did he get a good Navajo name?" She smiled and waited patiently, knowing that it usually took longer to receive an answer because the mother might be translating her question from English to Navajo in her mind, formulating an answer, and then translating it back into English.

"His name is Kee Nez," she said simply.

"Oh, I like the sound of that!" The enthusiasm in the woman's voice made her believable. "Doesn't Nez mean 'tall'?"

A proud smile and a nod from the new mother affirmed Alice's limited Navajo vocabulary.

"Would you like for me to pray for him?" Alice queried, knowing her chances were good for a favorable response.

The young mother shot a quick glance over at Grandma in the corner before nodding again. Grandma hadn't understood the question, but she might have something to say later. Still, she sensed that Grandma liked this woman, too, and she deeply wanted a blessing prayer for Kee. She gave Alice a slight nod.

"OK, let's pray . . . Father, thank You for this blessed day. Thank You for a beautiful baby! Lord, take good care of him always—bless him, bless his mother and grandmother with what they need in this life. And Lord, lead this little boy into a beautiful future in Your truth. Please, always be close to him, and may he know You. This is my prayer in the name of Jesus. Amen."

Alice opened her eyes, smiling. "Now. We've prayed, and God will bless. But remember, the best way to help your little one is to bring him over to church. You are always welcome there."

Then, as suddenly as she had come, Alice was bidding them farewell and heading out the door and down the hall to another room where an ailing Grandpa lay. The whole visit seemed to end on an abrupt and hasty note—the two Navajo women would never have gone about visiting friends that way. Still, there was something about Alice's inner sunshine that they craved. In silence, each woman reflected on the strange visit, though neither spoke of it again.

As they left the hospital the next day with a bundled-up Kee, a ray of light and an unforgotten prayer went with them. It was a prayer they would be needing soon enough.

The crisp air outside the hospital felt more natural to them as they crunched through the frozen snow toward a much-dented relative's pickup that waited for them in the small parking area. It felt good to have been in a helpful fragment of the Bilagana world, and it felt good to be heading back to their own way. But the warm environment behind them had been a positive interlude between the harsh realities of their lives, past and future.

CHAPTER 3

The Recurring Terror

"When my father and my mother forsake me, then the Lord will take me up" (Psalm 27:10).

GRANDMA, WHEN IS MY MOTHER coming back from the squaw dance?" Young Kee's eyes probed his grandma's wrinkled face in the light of the setting sun.

She sensed his loneliness as she closed the crude gate to the sheep pen. A private resentment of her daughter's frequent journeys away from their sheep camp flared within her heart. It was a part of her lifelong theme of abandonment that really involved many others besides her daughter.

When she was only 10, her mother had died in childbirth, and she, being the eldest, was left to care for her younger siblings. They all had been close during the years of their childhood; the struggle to survive had been shared by all. Even the youngest brother had learned how to search for the wild Navajo carrots and dig them out of the arid ground. Hunger had been a chronic theme when their dad went away to look for work and was gone for days at a time. But when they became adults, her siblings came around only when they needed something from her. Seldom did they show up to help her shear the sheep, repair her hogan, or work in the garden.

When a man began coming around and taking an interest in her, new hope sprang out of her woundedness. Some of the joy from her early childhood returned, and it remained beautiful until she conceived. Then the world changed again. By the time Kee's oldest aunt was born, the man

19

was gone, and another was visiting her hogan. This cycle of hope and loss continued over the years until she lost hope in men. Still, she allowed their entrance and exits over the years, nursing a bitter resentment in silence, grieving her losses in a quiet wellspring of sorrow. She longed for someone to be there for her yet the walls within her soul were very thick.

So her daughter's absence was only a continuation of the theme, and now another little person was suffering the consequences . . .

"One more day, maybe." She took her time before giving her brief answer. Other cultures would have assumed that she was not going to answer, but Kee had waited patiently.

"Grandma, some of the other kids have a dad who stays with them at their hogan. Where's my dad?"

She shot an unhappy glance at him. "I don't know. Come; let's carry some wood inside."

Kee had already heard that his dad was an important medicine man who rode a beautiful white horse over the rugged landscape to help in many ceremonies for sick and frightened people. Kee had been told that he wore shiny cowboy boots, a large silver concho belt, and lots of turquoise and silver around his neck and wrists. He had heard only a little bit about the tall, good-looking man. Though he could picture such a man in his mind, Kee had never seen him.

It seemed that his dad had had only one encounter with his mother. It had taken place in the nearby hills after a successful ceremony for her family. He had stayed around for a few days afterward, and then had been called away by another family in crisis—but not before Kee's conception had occurred. No one expressed any unhappiness about it. After all, they got Kee out of the deal, and the medicine man had helped them. Mother never said anything bad about the man. She missed him, and often went to the squaw dances, hoping to see him. She thought how honored she was to have been with such a man who was great among her people. While the squaw dances did not bring the two of them back together, they gave her other social contacts that she had missed during her younger days alone in the hills with the sheep. Holding hands with a man during the firelight dances was somewhat of an affirmation for her fragile ego. After all, she was now in her late 30s and still unclaimed.

But no one felt more cheated than Kee. He missed having a father a lot, and often looked carefully at tall strangers to see if any of them met the description he held in his heart. Like all boys, he searched for role models. It was many years before he found out the truth: his dad had died, but not before scattering a number of half brothers and sisters across the large reservation.

"When is Shichey [my grandpa] coming home? Is it the same day that my mother is coming?"

Grandma dropped the firewood next to the potbellied stove in the center of the hogan and turned toward the small boy. "Yes," she said.

"Will you tell me a story tonight?"

She smiled, showing the place where a front tooth was missing. "Maybe after I make some frybread."

Kee threw himself down on the low pile of sheepskins on which he would sleep. Only minutes before, Grandma had brought the skins inside. They had been airing out all day, stretched over the branches of the lone willow in the yard. They still had the fresh smell of the outdoors mixed with a trace of the familiar odor of sheep fat. A comfortable, dreamy feeling came over the boy as he buried his nose in the wool. His sheepskin bed had always been a safe place for him.

The sound of the crackling fire in the stove turned his attention back to Grandma, who had already formed the dough in a basin for the frybread. It always fascinated him to watch her take a piece of the dough, quickly shape it into a ball, and then throw it back and forth between her hands until it was a large, white tortilla. For Kee, this was love. The sight and sound of the dough clapping between her hands was an inner trigger for warm feelings in his heart. Once she had shaped it into an almost perfect circle as thin as a pizza crust, she eased it into the waiting kettle of hot oil on the stove. The dough made a loud popping sound as it sank into the oil, making his mouth water, because he knew the frybread was seconds away from being in his hands.

The hot, crunchy-on-the-outside-soft-on-the-inside bread was a satisfying meal for the two of them all by itself. When they had eaten all they wanted, they went outside the one-room structure and sat in the soft sand by Grandma's loom. The sky was clear, and the stars were incredibly bright—the perfect night for stories.

"I want to hear about the twins, my grandma!" Kee always wanted to hear about the twin heroes. Their adventures were fascinating, and their absent father gave him a connection with them that he could not verbalize.

"Maybe I will tell you about the time that the twins went up into the sky, looking for their dad," Grandma mused. She sensed that his questions about his dad were a sign that he might benefit from this part of the story.

"The twin boys were cared for by their mother, the white bead woman," she began. "This was the daughter of first man and first woman. When these boys where 15 days old, they were already young men. They were afraid to go to the south, west, or north because of the terror of the people-eating monsters. So they went east, chasing chickadees. It was then that Dotso, the great all-wise fly, told them that their dad was the sun. So the boys went home and told their mother that they wanted to go to their dad's home. They warned their mother, the daughter of first man and first woman, not to look at them as they left. Then they started out.

"When they left the hogan, they stood beside each other and lifted their right feet to take a step. When they did this, they stepped right onto a rainbow, and then to the top of the mountain, chol'i'i. Then they found that they were in a land of rolling sand, far to the east. They didn't know this place, but there was an old man there. He asked if they were the boys he'd heard about, the ones who were looking for their dad. When they told him yes, he vomited up something and told the boys to take it along with them. The old man was the worm with the sharp tail. He told them to use what he'd given them when their dad would test them with his tobacco. He warned them that their dad was very fierce, and that he would hurt them if they were not careful.

So the boys left the old man and continued on through many hardships. And when they were way, way to the east, they reached the door of a huge turquoise house—"

Grandma's story stopped abruptly, interrupted by a sudden spine-chilling call that pierced the night air. It came from a hilltop beyond the sheep pen.

"Yi-yi-yi-yi-yi-yi-yi-yi-yi!" There it was again.

Kee knew it was not the howl of a coyote. "skinwalker!" he whispered as he shot a fearful look at the old woman. Without another word, both of them rose and hurried into the hogan. The old door didn't seem secure enough, even after Grandmother bolted it with a piece of cedar wood. So she tied a rope to the door handle and anchored it to an old trunk on the opposite wall. The frightened pair then took positions on their respective sheepskin beds. The fire had died out, but neither felt motivated to do anything but listen and wait.

Even the dogs were strangely quiet. It was said that the skinwalkers have power over the dogs at times and can even change shape, change into a dog. However, those were actually cases of spiritual powers impersonating animals for an intimidating purpose. Kee had overheard a family member say that human skinwalkers could even blow powder on a person that would make them instantly go to sleep; it had happened before. He buried himself in the sheepskins, except for one ear and one eye. He scarcely breathed, straining every nerve toward any changes on the outside. With his half-concealed eye he glanced around the small, eight-sided room, wondering if the notched and interlocking logs would hold out the evil person.

Maybe it's going away, somewhere else! Kee thought hopefully.

Then he noticed that Grandma was sitting on top of her sheepskins, listening in the dark. She seemed calm but very still, like a guardian statue. That made Kee feel safer. He shifted his gaze upward to the smoke hole in the ceiling of the hogan. It was too small for anyone of normal size to pass through, but would a skinwalker be able to come in that way?

He didn't have long to wonder.

Outside, a frightening, monotonous chant from the direction of the sheep pen seemed to be coming closer. It continued for several long minutes then it stopped. Kee welcomed the silence but strained his ears even more in an effort to detect any subtle movement.

In a matter of seconds the hogan door squeaked faintly as cold fingers tested its lock, the chilled hand of a naked human under the control of an evil power. Then, as if they hadn't been terrified enough, the whole roof seemed to quake as the skinwalker swung himself up by a supporting beam to the top of the hogan. There were several thumps before the eerie silhouette of a coyote's head blotted out the stars that only a moment before had been shining in through the smoke hole in the ceiling.

Kee's heart rate surged, the loud pounding in his chest adding to his fears. Surely he would be located and cursed by the mere sound of his heartbeat!

Then a soft voice spoke across the room, and as hard as it was to tear his gaze from the hideous head in the smoke hole, he looked at Grandma.

She was praying earnestly, and while Kee could not remember later what she said, it was a positive distraction. Her gentle words seemed to take him away from the situation and into the presence of powers and authorities beyond the small players in this conflict. His mind filled with wonder to think of such great and holy beings. He wondered what they were like, and if they would help Grandma and him.

As Kee focused on Grandma and her prayer, the skinwalker seemed to sense that there was nothing to be gained with these two—for the time being anyway. There were other victims who were far easier. He slipped away so silently that at first neither Kee nor his grandma noticed he was gone.

When Kee forced himself to look again at the smoke hole, only stars in the night sky shone through. "He's gone!" he whispered hoarsely to Grandma.

But she continued her prayer as though she hadn't heard.

Only after the hogan felt safe and peaceful again did Grandma cease her prayer long enough to build up the fire in the stove. She seated herself and looked across at the little boy's form under the sheepskins. "We are OK now," she said simply. The dancing firelight came out of the cracks in the old stove and played on her wrinkled face and the log walls.

Kee watched until his heavy eyelids closed and released him to a happy dreamland. There had been enough trauma for one day, and now, in his dreams, the boy followed the soft, jumping lambs that eventually formed themselves into friendly, fluffy clouds in a turquoise sky.

CHAPTER 4

When Normal Is Strange

"Train up a child in the way he should go" (Proverbs 22:6).

"HERE; TAKE THIS FRYBREAD over to your auntie's hogan." Mother's directions were not too hard to follow, and young Kee was relieved that she was back home. Her absence only made him more desperate to make her happy so she wouldn't leave him again. His fifth birthday had passed uneventfully three months earlier.

Auntie's place was just over the hill, behind the big rocks. He knew that Auntie's new man, Tom, had been staying over there, too. Kee didn't have a good feeling about the man, but he loved being around his great auntie, Mary. She smiled whenever she saw Kee, and it made him feel special.

The narrow, dusty trail was well worn with the small hoof prints and the dry droppings of sheep. It had a soft, comfortable feel to it, and Kee's little moccasins made only slight marks among the sheep tracks. He squinted at the bright morning sky after a large crow flew overhead, croaking its warning. He remembered that his people were not fond of crows. The big bird glided silently away, and the small boy shifted his gaze back to the broom bushes immediately in front of him.

His fascination with the natural world made him forget that he still held the frybread until he rounded the big rock formation and began his final decent to Auntie's hogan. The open doorway faced the east, as every good Navajo home does, and today wild laughter rolled out from the shadows within. For some unexplainable reason, the sound gave Kee a strange twinge of fear. Auntie was a quiet woman, and though laughter was normally a welcome sound, he was unaccustomed to the high level in her voice. He paused before the doorway then proceeded in with his gift.

The home was without electricity, so the darkness inside the hogan made it difficult for him to see anything but the stove in the center of the room. He stood silently at the threshold, waiting to be invited in.

"Oh, derz my boy!" boomed Auntie. "Come in, my sonny!"

Ignoring the queer feeling in the pit of his stomach, he entered and paused, waiting for his eyes to adjust to the shadows.

"Come ober here, sonny! You got sometheen for me?" A loud giggle followed as Kee walked over to his auntie, sitting on an old wooden bench next to her man. "Frybread! Look, Tom; he brought me frybread!" Her weathered hands reached toward him. One took the bundle, and the other stroked his cheek and hair.

The touch seemed strange to Kee. Auntie had never touched him like that before. It felt nice, but this morning she was a different person. Her breath had a strong, offensive smell, and her movements were shaky and awkward. He stepped back, uncomfortable with this whole encounter.

"You want medicine? Tom, get him some medicine!" Auntie ordered.

Kee did not answer but noticed as Tom awkwardly reached toward a scuffed-up wooden trunk next to the bench. He opened the lid and produced a fancy bottle with a corked mouth and long neck. He pulled the cork and reached for a tin cup sitting on the ground.

As Tom shakily poured the dark contents of the bottle into the common cup, Kee watched with interest. He knew about medicine. That was the word that Grandma had used when she told about how she made the skinwalker go away. It was also the same word that was associated with his missing father. Medicine was a good thing in Kee's mind. He remembered the bottle of sweet soda pop he had enjoyed at the trading post, where his family went once a month to barter for their supplies. It had been a rare treat.

"Here!" Tom's trembling arm extended the tin cup toward the small boy.

Kee took it, looked at the dark liquid again, and quickly tipped the contents into his mouth. A bittersweet taste rushed to every corner of his mouth, and a warm feeling raced down his throat, followed by a sputtering cough. Tom and Auntie exploded in hysterical laughter, making Kee feel ashamed. As soon as he could stop coughing, he ran out of the hogan, their laughter ringing in his ears.

The little bushes and the soft sand seemed less magical to Kee somehow. He felt confused and betrayed by his auntie's strange behavior. He made his way back up the trail, around the rock formation. The warmth in his stomach from the drink increased and comforted him. His heart hurt, but his stomach felt good, a combination that he would know again one day. A dark door had been opened to him, a door that would become heavier and harder to close.

Later, he would be reminded of this event during many other encounters with alcohol in his family. It was inevitable. Alcohol was called "medicine," and with all the sadness in the hearts of his people, it had become a popular medicine. When there was no money to buy it, they would make their own brew. Kee sometimes hungrily watched as the cans of fruit, raisins, and other ingredients from the trading post were dumped into a barrel, where they would sit for days. Then, when the whole mixture had ripened, it was put through a crude, homemade distiller.

Usually Kee was not offered a drink, but he was always present when the grownups started drinking. It was free entertainment for him, just like the interesting movies he would later become involved with. Sometimes it was funny—and sometimes scary or sad—but always it was exciting.

Over time, Kee noticed the pattern that developed. The uncles, aunts, and cousins would start drinking. Then laughter would begin, starting with soft chuckles as the relatives made funny comments. Louder it grew, and more out of control, until someone took offense at a personal comment, became angry, and started a fight. Sometimes it was an uncle and a cousin, but it was not uncommon for a woman to get into the fray, as well.

At first these fights frightened Kee. But over time his sensitivity to them was reduced, and he actually tried to get to a good spot where he could be safe to watch the conflict. He liked seeing the funny, clumsy swings of an uncle, and the hilarious shrieks of an aunt as she swung a broom or bucket at her opponent.

Bruises and blood often resulted, and this bothered Kee whenever it was a family member he was fond of. But usually the wounds were considered nothing worth going to the hospital for. A missing tooth or a scar over the eyebrow was just part of life. People simply woke up the next morning and went about their business.

It would take many years for Kee to learn that there were other Navajo families who never had the experience of living in a home dominated by the addiction to alcohol, that healthy homes are free of addictions. But in his childhood, survival within the insanity was his only option.

Sometimes the alcohol was in control, and the relatives' lower nature would assert itself. Kee watched with interest as certain family members passed out while others, whose partners were unconscious, would slip away in pairs. Occasionally Kee would follow at a distance and observe activities that a child should never see. Another dark door opened in his mind.

On the morning after, if the alcohol was all gone, the wagon was frequently hitched up, and the adults climbed in slowly. The fresh wounds and hangovers made them move stiffly and kept their expressions wooden. Their guilt, pain, and shame from the night before needed further consolation. Indeed, their whole lives needed compensation for their losses. The insatiable desires of a lonely soul can drive one far in a search for more of what is only an illusion. Kee's heart sank. He knew where they were going and what they would want from him.

"Stay here and watch the sheep!" they told the little boy, who was now about 6 years old.

"OK," Kee responded. But as the wagon creaked away, he could not bear the thought of being alone. Suddenly he ran after them until he caught up with the wagon and jogged along beside it.

"Go back! Stay there!" they yelled as the wagon lurched and jounced along.

"All right!" Kee replied, continuing to run beside the wagon. Eventually the distance from the sheep camp increased to the point that it was obvious that he might as well ride in the wagon with everyone else, and then Kee was allowed to climb in.

Kee's mom planned to sell her beautifully woven rug at the trading post, and Grandma had some corn to trade. The entire family looked forward to the event, and each one had their mind full of memories of previous trips to this hub of Navajo activity and hopes about what they might enjoy on this visit. Life was slow and simple out at the sheep camp, and while it had it's rugged beauty, it often left a person eager for diversions. After the dealing for the rug and corn, the family's cash flow allowed them to acquire food and other needed supplies. It also put them in a position to either brew more alcohol, or to visit the bootlegger.

The trading post was a classic combination of grocery, hardware, and feed store, as well as art gallery, all gathered under one roof. The Navajos were grateful for all the conveniences and necessities provided by the White traders who lived on their land, but recently rumors were coming in about Navajo rugs that were being sold back East for 10 times the amount the weavers had received. This created a subtle resentment that festered in the Navajos' minds. Why should they get so little for their beautiful rugs, that took weeks to make, when the trader got so much more for them when he made his trip back East?

Kee had often seen his mother, grandma, and aunties shearing the sheep, carding the wool, picking the little plants used to dye the wool, dying the wool, and spinning the yarn. All this had to happen before the weaving could begin. Each rug was a unique creation from the heart of the weaver.

"The spider woman, she taught us," Grandma would say. "Someday I will take you over to Canyon de Chelly to see her. She turned into a big rock over there."

Though the thought scared him, Kee always wanted to go see the rock near Chinle, Arizona. But at his age, even going to the trading post was a huge event. It seemed to him that all the candy, toys, and pop in the world were there. Grandpa, Mom, or some other relative always got him something special. He learned early on that if anyone had money, the others would count on that person to share with the rest of them. Sometimes it was Grandpa's pension check for serving in World War II as a code talker against the Japanese. Sometimes there was a rug to sell. Other times there was something pretty to pawn so that the family could have money.

Every adult in Kee's family wore silver and turquoise jewelry, a sign of prosperity and their only bank account. Regular banks were scarce and impractical for the many families who lived from hand to mouth. Whenever they needed something they didn't have the cash for, one of them would pawn a concho belt, bracelet, or necklace at the trading post, and whatever they wanted was theirs! Sometimes it would take months to pay off the item, and the interest they were charged was outrageous, but it didn't matter. The jewelry was often a family heirloom and the last remaining gift that they had received from an older, now deceased relative. So no price was too much to pay to retrieve such jewelry from the pawn shelf.

The trader knew this, and sometimes his conscience would be pricked. Yet he excused it as the reward of his small business out in this bleak and lonely country. He also thought that charging 20 percent interest might eventually teach these Navajos to make better financial choices for themselves. Even now banks are few in Navajoland, and the complexity of a checking account is overwhelming to many of the older ones.

But for Kee, none of this mattered. The trading post was the center of the world. Often he would journey in his mind down the aisles, remembering the fascinating utensils, toys, and yummy treats. It was a full day of jouncing and bouncing to reach the trader's home and store, and when they arrived, they would all sleep together in a drafty shelter on some straw near where the horses were tied. It was fun for the little boy! He felt secure as he snuggled in the middle of all his relatives. Everyone was sober, and even great auntie's snoring didn't bother him.

One particular trip stuck in Kee's mind because, on the way home, the man whom he called his grandpa, surprised him. As they headed the creaking wagon toward home, Grandpa reached into his pocket and handed Kee a piece of candy that he had refused to buy for him earlier. He had turned the little boy down at the trading post, saying he didn't have any more money.

"Did you find some money, my grandpa?"

Grandpa was slow to respond, and when he did he was very brief. "No."

"Then how did you get it?"

Silence followed, but Kee pressed the issue until Grandpa answered. "It jumped into my hand. Your mother didn't get enough money—the trader cheated her. So I got something more for her rug when he wasn't lookin'." Grandpa then unceremoniously passed around an assortment of candy to the rest of the passengers.

No one else commented, and Kee asked no more questions. But inside he thought about what Grandpa had said. In the years that followed, Grandpa's example helped to cement a philosophy that soon became his own. It made sense that stealing was OK when there was a good reason for it.

So Kee enjoyed the candy Grandpa had given him even more. It was like a trophy taken in battle. He now had someone to admire for his cleverness in taking back from the White trader what was rightfully his. Grandpa was his hero, and when he grew older he would tell Kee, "It's OK to steal sometimes. You can even cheat on your woman sometimes. Sometimes they will cheat on you, too. But you have to be strong and not do a bad thing if she does."

CHAPTER 5

A Journey Into the Pain

"The thing which I greatly feared is come upon me" (Job 3:25).

NOT LONG AFTER THE trading post trip Kee was inside the hogan with his mother. She had wearied of her wanderings and seemed resolved to stay put for a while. Seated on a freshly aired-out sheepskin, she was busy sorting the plants she had gathered to make special dyes for her wool.

Kee was proud of his mother's weaving. At the moment he was celebrating the joy her presence brought to his heart by beating on a pot near the doorway, as he had seen medicine men do, and was enjoying his version of their chants. In the middle of his concert he looked out the door just in time to see a frightening figure approaching. The tall, masked person, scantily dressed in a strange loincloth, carried grass and what looked like a rattle in his hands. His grayish skin contrasted with the feathers that adorned his head and wrists.

Kee quickly jumped up, slammed the door shut, and bolted it. "My mother!" he exclaimed. "skinwalker is out there!"

The masked figure drew nearer and shook his small rattle. Mother peered out a crack in the door then turned suddenly, smiling, and walked over to an old coffee can nestled among her weaving things. Reaching into the can, she made a clinking sound as her fingers extracted a silver dollar. "That's not a skinwalker, Kee—it's a ye bich'e! He's a holy being. He's coming for a gift. Here; give him this."

Kee closed his fist over the coin, hesitating. He'd been told about the ye bich'e, and about the time in the fall season when the snakes go underground. He didn't want to see the creature, let alone give it something.

But there was a knocking sound at the door, and Mother was scooting him over to it and undoing the bolt. Kee leaned against Mother, resisting her gentle force that was propelling him forward. His mild resistance ended in a frozen stare at the creature, now inches away and towering above him. No one had told him that ye bich'e was only a human dressed in this special way for ceremonies. To Kee, this fellow looked like one of the mythical monsters that had eluded the Twins after they got their lightning arrows from their father, the Sun.

"Give him your gift!" Mother urged. She was adamant that Kee should enter this part of the Navajo culture.

Kee, however, was too frightened to move. He stood transfixed, gazing at the sunlight on a tuft of dry grass on the ground behind the strange person. So Mother reached down, grabbed his hand, and extended it toward the being. Kee felt large fingers tug on the coin, and he released it. Then Mother was releasing him and closing the door behind them. She didn't blame him for his fright—she remembered when she first had seen a ye bich'e.

"Now that we gave him that gift we will have good fortune in this coming year," she promised.

But there would be no good fortune for Kee that year. Mother was already making plans to put him into school. The local Bureau of Indian Affairs boarding school seemed to be the obvious choice, as this would keep Kee busy and give her more free time during the week days.

Schools were better than they used to be. Only a couple generations before, Navajo children had been harshly rounded up and shipped off to designated Indian schools hundreds of miles from their homes for an education in the White man's ways, in spite of their parents' efforts to protect them from the atrocities of those institutions. It had been a barbaric way to civilize a defeated culture. But now boarding schools were a fact of life, and Kee's mother could see the personal benefits of having the federal government training her child. She told herself it wasn't so bad, now that the boarding school was right in Navajoland. She wasn't happy with the continuous burden of mothering, and this was an easy way out for her.

Tribal societies often shared the responsibility of child rearing among the extended family members, but Kee's mother had another complication. Another little life stirred within her now, and she didn't want to be overwhelmed by having an older, needy sibling in addition to her newest arrival. There was also a new man in her life, and he wanted to share her one-room hogan. Kee would simply have to find his own way through this "school of hard knocks."

▼▼▼

The nearest boarding school was not that many miles away, and its fresh beige paint job gave it an almost positive appearance as the ancient pickup rattled its way to the front office.

"I'll see you on the weekend when your uncle picks you up," Mother said. Then the old pickup roared out of the parking area.

A bewildered 6-year-old Kee watched until the pickup disappeared in a cloud of dust then he looked up at the boarding school principal who stood beside him. He did not look like a nice man, Kee thought, even when he was smiling. It seemed to be a strange, mechanical smile that covered something dark and frightening within. He was Bilagaana (White), and the only other Bilagaana Kee had known was the man who ran the trading post. Both men had the same detached air about them, but at least the trader occasionally gave him a piece of candy.

"Well, Kee, let's take your things over to your new home!" The principal's suggestion started a mental argument in Kee's mind as he shuffled along behind the well-dressed man.

"This is *not* my home," Kee muttered softly. "I already *have* a home up by the mesa."

The dormitory turned out to be a sequence of rooms filled with boys of all ages. Kee was assigned a bed and introduced to a short, chunky man, from some other tribe, who was the dean of the boys' quarters. He carried a thick, wooden paddle strapped to his belt. The principal then left, and Kee didn't see him again until much later. The dean gave Kee information about mealtimes and his rules.

"No fighting, no stealing, no Navajo language, and no gum in the dormitory," he concluded, his fingers tapping his paddle threateningly. "Remember that and you'll be OK."

With that the dean retreated to his quarters.

Immediately the other boys in the room started in on Kee. "Hey, baby face, where you from?" one roommate teased. "Look!" exclaimed another. "His face looks like nageezi [a pumpkin]!"

A loud chorus of laughter broke out among Kee's roommates. All of them were older than he was, and even though he was tall for his age, most of them were taller. Kee had never been around children such as these. His shy cousins were playful, but not like this. He felt embarrassed and sat on his bed, staring down at his dusty moccasins.

"Is he gonna cry?" one boy wondered aloud in a mocking tone.

"No," another decided. "At least not until tomorrow morning."

"Oh, yeah!" chimed in others. "Tomorrow he will!"

Kee hardly heard their comments as he struggled to control his feelings of abandonment and hurt. His family had always encouraged him to be strong. They had already taught him not to be a crybaby. But this was the hardest thing he had ever faced. The pain in his heart seemed to intensify with every passing minute until it was an ache that was almost too much to bear.

Fortunately, the supper bell rang just then, and all the boys rushed off to the cafeteria. Kee remained on his bed. He had no appetite. His hunger was in his heart. He missed his family, and it made all other hungers insignificant. But the dean, making his way to the cafeteria, noticed the boy on his bed and made him come to supper.

That night the boys started in on Kee again. They reminded him about the next morning, and Kee began to wonder what they meant. Surely no one could know what tomorrow would be like! Perhaps he would wake up and his mother would be there to take him home. When the lights went out, he buried his head in the pillow and finally gave in to the tears that had been waiting all day to come.

Morning began when the sky was barely gray. Kee felt himself being jerked roughly out of bed.

"Get up, baby face!" a big boy ordered. "Time for you to fight!"

Kee was dragged to a larger room where other big boys were bringing smaller boys from other rooms. Soon there was a crowd of big boys pushing little boys into the center of the room.

"OK, you two fight, or we'll beat you up!" commanded one of the biggest boys, pointing to two confused little boys.

The boys looked at each other in fear. Neither one wanted to fight. Indeed, they were barely awake! Nevertheless, they clenched their fists and began swinging at each other in earnest. Before long, one of the little fellows was crying and the fight was over. The boys laughed and teased the weaker child.

Then Kee was being pushed toward the little boy who had been victorious.

"OK," said a rough voice behind him, "now fight, baby face, or I'll beat you up bad!"

Kee looked fearfully at the other child, but the victor was no longer afraid. He was the winner and had some confidence under his belt. He glared at Kee, then peppered him with punches before he could prepare to defend himself. Disoriented, Kee raised his hand to defend his face, but the blows came too fast and too furiously. He made a couple halfhearted swings, then began to cry.

"See?" the voice behind him croaked. "A baby-faced crier!"

"A baby-faced crier!" chanted the others. "A baby-faced crier!"

More fights were forced on the smaller boys, and Kee was made to fight once again before the breakfast bell rang. He tried to fight, because he had seen what happened to one little boy who failed to fight. That child was punched, slapped, and kicked by the bigger boys for a long time. Even so, Kee lost that fight, too. He had no spirit to fight.

The rest of the day passed uneventfully. Only his bruises and the occasional name calling reminded him of how this day had started. The classroom time was better because at least there was a teacher in the room to protect Kee from the older children.

That afternoon one of the big boys made the mistake of beating up another child in front of the dean's apartment window. The dean stormed out, paddle in hand, and made the big boy pull his pants down and receive eight hard strokes on his bare bottom. The big boy didn't cry out, but Kee saw tears in his eyes and a smile of shame as he pulled his pants back up.

Everything was confusing to Kee, and as he thought about it he came to some conclusions. It was OK for adults to hit people, but kids must not. If he fought in front of the dean, it was bad; and if he fought in front of the boys, it was good—if he won. Tomorrow morning was a dreadful thought, but he resolved to be ready.

That night his pillow was wet again with tears of longing for his home and family.

Kee didn't know that other little boys were also quietly shedding their own tears that night. The ache in his heart was so strong and all encompassing, yet his fear of another day of this harshness distracted him from all-out grief. He thought about the moves of the boys who had successfully fought that morning. He remembered how they had held their fists and struck out quickly. As he dozed off, his arm gave a sudden jerk as he pictured himself fighting in his dreams.

The next day offered a respite from the pre-breakfast violence. Instead of the older boys shaking him awake, the dean strode across the room, whacking the bedposts with his paddle and calling out an announcement for the mid-week early morning chapel time. "Get up and dress quickly," he ordered. "All of you must go to a chapel meeting before you can go to breakfast. Catholics to the library, and Protestants to the gym!"

Kee had no idea what the dean's words meant, but he understood that the sharp crack of his paddle and the order to get dressed quickly must be taken seriously. As he hustled into his clothing, he noticed that many of the boys were heading toward the gym not because they were Protestant, but because it was closer to the cafeteria. Kee followed them and was surprised to see a happy-looking man standing by the door, shaking each boy's hand and giving out song books. Girls filed in on the other side of the gym, accepting a handshake and a song book from a friendly woman, who was standing by their door.

Then the smiling man picked up a guitar, and soon a most wonderful sound came out of the instrument! Kee had heard and enjoyed only the chants of the Navajo singers and the static-filled songs of his uncle's old radio in the pickup. This was more wonderful than anything else! The songs were in English, of course, but it didn't matter.

After the songs, the man put his guitar down and told a story about a man who loved everybody and did amazing things. Kee was very interested in the story. Love was not a common theme in the tales of the Twin heroes. A loving man was a special thought for the fatherless boy.

There was only one bad incident that day. When a teacher heard a boy say something in Navajo, all the boys in the school were called together. They formed two lines about three feet apart and were told to pull their belts off. Then the unfortunate child was made to run between the two lines while the other boys all took swings at him with their belts. It was a long line, and the boy was struck many times. When the boy came close to Kee, he saw that he was crying as he ran. It bothered his conscience, and he made only a halfhearted attempt to hit him as he passed.

This incident also confused Kee. He had been raised to feel special for being Diné, but here the language of his people was not acceptable. Since he spoke very little English, he was terrified that he might slip up. Once, when the teacher asked him a question, Kee hadn't understood. All he knew was that he must not speak in Navajo. In shame and fear he put his head down and stared at his pencil. The teacher had waited a moment then impatiently moved on. Kee was spared from further trouble.

That night the boys began talking about the fights that would occur the next morning. Kee knew there would be no chapel for another week. He wished every morning had a chapel, with that friendly Bilagaana and his guitar. He drifted back and forth between the morning service and picturing himself fighting with his quick moves. Eventually the fights won out and followed him into his dreams.

Kee awoke to the squeaking of bed springs as the big boy rolled out. Morning had come. Since the dean came out early only on chapel day, there would be no avoiding the rough treatment this day. Kee pulled himself out of bed.

The boys were gathering in the larger room. Kee was one of the first to be picked for a fight. His opponent was about his size, and before he could get his guard up Kee hit him with a flurry of punches. The boy swung wildly once then began to cry.

"Hey! Baby face is a good fighter!" exclaimed a bigger boy. "Let him fight another one!"

The next boy was the same one who had beat Kee up previously. Glaring at Kee, he charged in, peppering his face with punches. Somehow Kee managed an uppercut that caught the other boy on the chin. Stunned, he stepped back, and Kee pressed forward with his own barrage of punches. The child covered his face with his hands, but Kee didn't let up until he was crying loudly.

"Hey, a new champ!" cheered the bigger boys. They enjoyed the power of making the little boys hurt each other. Kee discovered that he liked the admiration he got when he was winning. He was only matched against one other boy that morning, and he won that fight just as easily.

The weekend finally arrived, and his uncle's old pickup rattled into the parking area. Kee had been waiting for a couple hours after the last class. His uncle was often late, but when Kee saw him, it didn't matter. He was going home!

Back at the sheep camp the only ones who seemed really happy to see him were his grandma and grandpa. They smiled, and Grandma gently patted him on the back. Mother seemed occupied with the new man, whom Kee disliked. No one asked him about his week, but Kee wanted to forget it anyway. He was so happy to be home that he even greeted the dogs with a handshake.

Before he knew it, the weekend was over and he was being loaded back into the pickup, despite his protests. He didn't go into details. That wasn't the way of his people. But Kee made it clear what he wanted. "It's bad over there," he cried. "Let me stay!"

The only answer he got was the closing of the pickup door by his mother. She did try to encourage him by reminding him about the coming weekend. But Kee knew he needed an intervention sooner than that. All the way back to the school he made note of certain landmarks and the way the road went.

That evening the boys in the dorm said they were going to change the fighting rules. They were going to make the champions fight the bigger boys. It was the final push that Kee needed. He knew the way home, and he wasn't going to stay around for any more of this. He crept out of the sleeping quarters and headed for the bathroom. After relieving himself, he climbed out the window. How cool the night air felt after the stuffy dorm rooms that always smelled like dirty socks!

Kee traveled quickly, his heart feeling lighter with each step. By the time the skies turned gray, he was within sight of the mesa. Not until he saw the hogan did he begin to think of what he would say.

"Good morning, my mother!" he greeted.

"No good," she chided. "You're supposed to be at school! I'm not happy about you coming here."

Kee remained calm. He had heard this sort of thing before, and he knew that it would not get any worse. He headed for the wood pile. Gladly, he gathered firewood and brought it inside the hogan. Then he went out to the garden. Grandpa's corn was harvested, and now he was making a fire for his stone and mud oven where he would soon steam it. "Hello, my grandpa!"

"Hello, my grandson!" Grandpa answered enthusiastically. "Did dose Bilagaanas do a bad thing?"

Kee smiled at him. It was clear that Grandpa, at least, was OK with his not going to school. "Yes!" he replied simply. He decided to stick closer to his grandpa. If he did, perhaps he wouldn't be so likely to be sent back to school. About noon, though, a white vehicle approached the camp, trailing a cloud of dust.

"BIA school jeep," Grandpa warned softly. "They are coming for you!"

Kee needed no further warning. He turned and ran for the mesa. He was a good runner. Grandpa had trained him many times before by making him run with water in his mouth, then spitting it out when he reached the finish line. It was a hard way to run, but now it paid off. By the time the jeep stopped by the hogan the boy was halfway up the mesa and still running. The chubby man in the jeep visited with Mother awhile then headed back toward the school.

When he reached the top, Kee continued running until he was out of sight among the junipers and pines. His heart slowed its hasty strokes as he walked further toward the center of the mesa. He had been up there many times before with the sheep. He knew where to go. He was frightened but victorious as he drank from a hidden spring in the afternoon sun. Its small, shallow pool comforted him, and he decided to spend the night there. He thought of his hunger and began gathering pinion nuts from under the trees. He had filled all his pockets and munched considerably by the time he returned to the spring. He didn't know how to make a fire without matches, but decided he didn't want to risk attracting any visitors anyway. He curled up in the tall grass, pulling some of the stalks over himself to ward off the fall chill. It was a peaceful night, interrupted only by the deer breaking twigs as they visited the spring for their nightly drink.

The next morning Kee was awakened by an aching hunger and the fall chill. He imagined the fry bread crackling in the hogan and headed off the mesa. Suddenly he stopped—the white jeep was in the camp again! The chubby man was talking to Mother. He didn't know that she had told the man to come back and catch Kee early in the morning. She hadn't expected him to spend the night on the mesa. He sat down by a juniper and waited for the jeep to leave. The blue juniper berries were not the sweetest, but they took the edge off his hunger as he watched the events playing out down below.

When the jeep had gone, Kee continued his descent and made for Grandpa in the garden. *"Ya'at'eeh,* my grandpa!"

"Ya'at'eeh, my grandson!" Grandpa hadn't lost any of his enthusiasm. "You tricked 'em again!"

"Did you go to a school, Grandpa?"

"Yes," Grandpa said slowly, "but I couldn't run away when they sent me to Oklahoma. That's worse than the school here."

"Where's that one, Grandpa?"

"Way over there." Grandpa pointed in typical Navajo style, his lips protruding in the direction that he wanted Kee to look. It was not polite to point the finger. "It takes one day to get to Gallup, then two days on the bus to get to that school in Oklahoma."

Kee hadn't known about this part of his grandpa's past. Suddenly he was immersed in thoughts of Grandpa's similar experience in a place that was too far away to return home. A new, unspoken bond was formed between the two though neither said any more about it.

"You see that yellow bird over there?"

Kee's eyes followed the general trajectory of Grandpa's pointing lips to a far corner of the garden area. He spotted the bird and nodded.

"That yellow bird," Grandpa continued, "the medicine men need for some of their ceremonies. They pay good money for it!"

"How can I get it?" Kee inquired. "Do I shoot it with an arrow?"

"No. Later on, when we finish here, we'll make a trap."

Kee smiled up at the man he called "my grandpa." Actually, by strict Navajo definition, he was not. He was merely the latest man that his grandma had become involved with. But it didn't matter to Kee. He was very fond of his elder and learned many things from him. In return, Kee gave the old man an attitude of respect that had been missing in his life. They were a team. Whenever the white jeep appeared on the horizon,

Kee acted on a subtle hint from Grandpa and would be on his way up the mesa. An entire semester passed without the trauma of boarding school.

But pleasant things often come to an end. Kee didn't know that the Bureau of Indian Affairs had him on their wanted list. Early one January morning, while the sun was still struggling to overcome the darkness, the hogan door flew open, and two grown men with a new rope burst in. Kee had no time to notice that Mother didn't seem too surprised. The men pounced on him and quickly tied him up. Kee kicked, bit, and fought with all his might, but it was hopeless. The men carted him out like a small bundle of firewood and sat him between them inside the cab of the white pickup.

As they drove off only Grandpa seemed upset. "You do a bad thing! You cannot make him Bilagaana!" was all he said to Kee's mother before stomping off. She shrugged and went on nursing her new baby.

Inside the pickup Kee was getting a lecture from the Navajo driver. "Your game is over! We are taking you to a school that is farther away— to Chinle. And if you run away from there, we now have horses to ride and can follow you up the mesa. So we'll catch you again, and then we'll send you to Oklahoma! Don't run away from Chinle—you don't ever want to go to Oklahoma. There are other tribes there, and they don't like us Navajos."

Kee made no response, but he had heard and understood. He was too hurt and angry. Chinle was less than 100 miles from his beloved mesa in the heart of Navajoland. He resigned himself to the fact that he would have to stay at school. Tears silently coursed down his cheeks, and inside his heart the little boy imposed a prison sentence upon himself. He would stay in the Chinle boarding school. He never wanted to have to go to Oklahoma.

CHAPTER 6

The Widening Ditch

"I looked for a man . . . [to] stand . . . in the gap . . . but I found none"
(Ezekiel 22:30, NIV).

GRANDPA WATCHED THE CLOUD of dust growing smaller in the distance. The white pickup seemed in a big hurry. He silently fought a battle with hopelessness, and finally won. His heart ached at the thought of what Kee must now endure, but he knew the boy would not forget what he had learned. He remembered his own childhood of suffering and thought about how he himself had prevailed against the system. The flame of rebellious pride flared up within him. He had won his battle of passive resistance with a dominant culture.

Now it was Kee's turn.

In Chinle, Kee arrived at the boarding school in time to join the other children for breakfast. Although he was upset about being forced to attend school, he did like the variety offered at the cafeteria. It was very different from his traditional food. He especially liked all the sweet things on the menu.

As it turned out, the Chinle dormitory had better supervision. The dean and his assistants were more watchful, and much of the abuse was held in check. Kee was relieved that he was not a regular victim of the older boys, and he had an easier time concentrating in the classroom, even if the Navajo language was not permitted.

Kee especially liked the Wednesday chapel service each week, which was similar to the one in the other school. He figured that the Protestant chapel was right for him because of his previous experience with that friendly man with the guitar. But in Chinle the Protestants didn't bring a guitar. Still, Kee enjoyed their stories. He was fascinated by the Creator who had come down to die for His creatures and wondered why his grandma had never told him that beautiful story.

The other thing Kee enjoyed about Chinle was the amazing Canyon de Chelly (pronounced *dishay*). The boarding school staff frequently loaded the children on the bus and drove them to a parking area where they could hike down a narrow trail to the bottom where Anasazi ruins lay by a stream on the canyon's floor. The ancient pueblo walls looked frightening to Kee. He'd been told that bad spirits lived in those places. The Anglo staff members didn't seem to be afraid. They walked close to the ruins, and some of them poked around, looking for artifacts. But whenever Kee reached that spot he always turned and headed back up the trail. There were many other places to explore.

One sunny day the staff decided to take the children up del Muerto, one of de Chelly's side canyons. When the buses stopped among the thickly growing junipers and pinion pine, the children poured out into the fresh air and were led to the rim. From that vantage point they could look at a downward angle at a high sandstone shelf some 600 feet above the canyon floor. Though it had only an overhanging rim, it was called a cave—Massacre Cave. One of the few Native teachers explained that they were looking at a place where 25 Navajos had tried to hide from Spanish soldiers in 1805. However, they had been spotted, and the soldiers rifles had pinned them down behind boulders on the ledge that was no more than eight feet wide. Other soldiers climbed up a sheer cliff, almost 600 feet high, to slaughter them with swords and knives.

Another teacher offered his binoculars to anyone who wanted to look at the narrow shelf on which white, sun-bleached bones still could be seen. Kee noted the man's morbid fascination with the bones but took the binoculars in an effort to satisfy his own curiosity. He thought of what Grandpa had always said about staying away from the dead but reasoned within himself that this was far away from the place of the dead, and therefore OK. Kee saw many small bones among the many bleached remains.

"Did they kill children?" he asked.

"There were women, children, and old people trying to hide there," replied the teacher. "They were all killed, and their ears were cut off."

"Why?"

"Their ears were taken to the Spanish governor in Santa Fe, along with the ears of about 59 other Navajos, as proof of the soldiers' success."

Pain and anger welled up in Kee. The thought of his people dying so helplessly at the cruel hands of the Spanish sickened him. All the other stories that Grandpa and Grandma had told him about the twin heroes could not console his spirit. Bitterness brewed in his heart as he rode back to school. It was a wound that would take years to heal.

The buses took the children back to the canyon many times, but never again to del Muerto. Gradually, Kee got over his sickened feelings at the canyon. After all, his people had managed to survive, and now this place was theirs by decree of the United States government. The cottonwoods, sheep pens, and hogans with their peach trees dotted the canyon floor, just as they had for hundreds of years.

Kee noticed that there were Navajo runners on the trail. They reminded him of his own runs up the mesa at home. It gave him a familiar, inspired feeling, and on his next canyon trip, he began running down the trail. It gave him a sense of freedom and exhilaration that he had never enjoyed before. When he had run for Grandpa it was a serious test, and he had been afraid of disappointing the old man. Winded, he reached the floor of the canyon and stopped to rest. Other runners he had noticed also ran up the trail. He resolved to build up his strength and pictured a time when he would run all the way down and all the way back up the canyon trail without stopping.

This resolve motivated Kee to run harder on the school grounds. He ran even when the children were not required to, and the more he ran the freer he felt. His grades improved, and his loneliness became less pronounced. He found friends among the little boys who helped him hang on until his first school break.

Back at the sheep camp below the mesa nothing had changed. Kee's mother was weaving another rug and barely had time to greet him with a twinkle in her eyes. Her man was outside by a fire, doing the ancient work of a silversmith. He had no interest in Kee, and the boy wasn't drawn toward him, either. He strolled slowly toward Grandma's hogan with an awkward feeling in his heart. Didn't anyone know how much it meant to him to be home again? Didn't anyone feel the same way?

Finding Grandma's place empty, he set out to see where the rest of the family was. Squinting against the bright sun, he scanned the countryside around him. Up at the top of the mesa's edge he spotted Grandpa on horseback with the sheep. Breaking in a loping run, he made for the base of the mesa. Without a pause, the boy reached the steep incline and continued to run even as he ascended.

Grandpa watched with pleasure as the child made his way up the mesa. He had never seen Kee do such a thing before. When he arrived at the top, Grandpa offered a simple, hearty *"Ya'at'eeh!"*

Kee grinned. It felt good to be back, yet his heart still lacked something. When the school break was over, Kee made no protest about going back. He was ready to return and enjoy his friends at Chinle. He realized now that his own little buddies and adventures were just as interesting as anything at home. The wonder of discovery and his own inner need now led him in an ever-widening circle, beginning a pattern that Kee managed to maintain over a number of years. School life, with its own flurry of work and activities, was punctuated by memorable breaks back home. Some of these were common, everyday events—sitting on a rock, watching the sheep nibble grass; trapping coyotes; watching Grandma weave her latest rug; and helping Grandpa shear the sheep.

Kee especially remembered his first squaw dance. It was impressive to see the men, galloping on horses toward the dance area, carrying partly unwound bolts of colored cloth that streamed along behind them like long, low-flying flags. Grandpa had explained that this dance was actually a ceremony called "The Enemy Way," because it was for veterans who returned from war. "Dis way the spirits of da dead enemies don't bother da men when dey come home," he explained. "Der minds get away from da enemy spirits."

Kee had sensed the importance of this gathering. It made him feel proud of his people and their ways. But his mood changed later when he noticed that Grandma had taken the hand of another man in the actual squaw dance. Quickly he looked over at Grandpa and saw him in the firelight, watching the dancers before turning and walking away into the darkness. Kee remembered his words: "You must be strong, because sometime your woman may go away with some other man." A sick and painful feeling came over the boy. But he stayed in the circle of light, watching in horrified fascination as Grandma went around the circle with the strange man. She was smiling in a way that he had never seen before. It seemed to go on forever, but it was only a few minutes before the dance was over, and she was rejoining Kee and his mother. Everything was normal again, and Kee could not understand why it had bothered him so much. He thought little more about it until much later.

▼ ▼ ▼

In the ever-turning cycles of the seasons Kee continued to grow. He always had been tall for his age, and as he entered the teen years he was one of the first in his class to reach the six-foot mark. This advantage diminished the number of physical attacks he received. Life became less frightening and exploration became his first passion. He already knew almost every nook and cranny in his beloved mesa, but this only drove him into wider circles of discovery whenever he had a school break.

Once, while riding Grandpa's horse on top of an adjacent mesa a few miles from the sheep camp, he found an odd looking shed the size of a small doll house. It was locked, but Kee managed to pry the little door open by using a wooden post and some leverage.

The contents of the little shed were mysteriously familiar to Kee. He remembered the firecrackers that Grandpa had gotten him once when they had sold a beautiful rug at the trading post. The objects in the shed looked like giant firecrackers with fuses that were many feet long. What Kee didn't know was that the Bureau of Indian Affairs sometimes stored dynamite there for future projects. The young teen cautiously unwound one of the fuses. "It must be long because this kind makes a big noise," he reasoned, and he went to work laying it out on the ground outside the shed. The stick of dynamite was left inside the shed.

Instinctively he sensed that this was not something he wanted to be caught doing. So as he carefully surveyed his deadly handiwork, Kee thought of a plan: An older cousin-brother lived about a quarter of a mile away. He would light the long fuse, jump on the horse, and ride to his relative's camp.

With trembling hands he lit one of the wooden matches he had snitched from the can on the shelf in Mother's hogan. The gentle breeze did not succeed in putting it out, and the fuse began to burn. Quickly Kee jumped on the horse and galloped off toward his cousin-brother's house. He slowed the pace before emerging from the thick juniper trees and trotted up to the hogan. His relative and three older men were sitting at a table outside, drinking coffee. The gentle morning sunlight made the scene a tranquil one as Kee hopped off his horse, greeted them, and sat down at the table.

The burning fuse was in his mind as he listened to their conversation. In deference to one of the men, who was of Mexican descent, they spoke in English. Old Man Yazzie was telling about one of his nephews who, under the cover of a snowstorm, had gone to the nearby Hopi Indian reservation the past winter to steal some of their horses. "He neber came back," Old Man Yazzie reported. "I tink doze Hopis got him, and dey—"

BOOM!

The explosion shook the mesa and made Old Man Yazzie spill his coffee on himself. Grandpa's horse shied, and the dogs started barking.

"Aw!" Old Man Yazzie exclaimed. "What was dat?"

The surprised and bewildered old men made it doubly hard for Kee to keep a straight face. He put his head down with his hand over his face in an attempt to hide his smile.

"Hey!" yelled cousin-brother. "How come you came riding here in a big hurry? Did you do something to dat little BIA house?"

Kee could bear it no longer. Laughter tumbled out of him, and it was joined by laughter from the other four. Despite their scare it had been a good joke because nobody liked the BIA anyway.

Kee rode home with a merry heart. It was the last day of the school break, and he was trying to make it last forever. He didn't know this would be his last ride on the mesa for a very long time.

Back at school his newfound sense of humor was challenged right away. Lucinda, a girl who liked him, began teasing him. She had always liked him but didn't know how to show it. Her attempts to get his attention were limited to name calling and jabbing him from behind as they sat in class. Outwardly, Kee had tolerated Lucinda's actions patiently. But inside he was seething over it. It was not an anger he could clearly sense until it would rise up in a moment of rage at an abusive act.

One such act awaited Kee in the first class after the school break. He had taken his assigned seat in front of Lucinda, and almost immediately she had set in on him. "Hey," she whispered, "derz something on da back of your shirt!"

The teacher had taken attendance and was busily writing the first math problem on the chalkboard. Kee tried to ignore Lucinda, but he began to feel the anger rising.

"It's a dirty spot right dare!" she said and jabbed him in the back with her freshly sharpened pencil.

Kee usually took her overtures stoically, but this time something snapped. He whirled around and cuffed Lucinda's face with the back of his hand just as the teacher turned around.

"Kee Nez!" the man spoke sternly. "You will be punished at recess, but for now come sit in the corner!"

Kee complied without any excuses. He had seen this teacher in operation before. It was his first offense, but he knew it wouldn't matter. The typical punishment this man administered was six or seven strokes with his heavy yardstick. The worst thing about it was that the whole class was usually watching outside the building, through the large windows. Kee remembered the numerous times he and the others had laughed at some student in the unfortunate spot that he now occupied. The thought of that much shame was unbearable, and Kee decided he would not allow it to happen.

When the noon hour arrived and all the students except Kee were dismissed, the teacher called Kee over to his desk. Out of the corner of his eye he could already see his classmates gathering outside the window. Even Lucinda was there, smiling. The volcano of anger with its deadly hot lava began to seethe within him again. As Kee approached the teacher and his punishment tool, he decided on a course of action. Quickly, he jerked the yardstick out of the man's hand, snapped it in two over his own thigh, and rushed to the window where he threw the two pieces out at his classmates.

"Young man"—the teacher's iron grip on his arm could not be ignored—"you are coming to the principal's office with me!"

Kee meekly followed the teacher's lead. He had preserved his honor and that was what really mattered to him. Once inside the principal's office, Kee drifted in and out of the teacher's exaggerated tirade about his violence toward other students, open defiance toward his teacher, and his damage to the teacher's private property. His mind wandered from wondering which type of punishment they would give him to the gentle breeze coming in the window to the angry teacher's words.

The principal calmly listened until the teacher had finished. He already knew, from Kee's file, about his truancy at the other boarding school. "Well, young man," the principal began, a tone of condescending sadness in his voice. "You don't seem to appreciate your opportunity to receive an education on your own reservation. You leave me with no choice— I'm going to have to send you to Oklahoma!"

Kee took the news in stunned silence. He had thought that maybe he would have to go through the gauntlet of belts on the playground or maybe have to clean the toilets for a month. But never had he thought of going to Oklahoma. It was the unthinkable, his ultimate fear. A sinking feeling of helpless dread came over him.

He was pushed toward a chair while phone calls and arrangements were made. Before he knew it, two men in a white pickup were waiting for him outside. They would take him to Gallup, where he would then be put on a bus for Oklahoma. Kee moved in a passive daze. He felt too numb to resist or do anything to change his situation. However, that numbness would go away soon enough.

CHAPTER 7

Band-aids for the Soul

"A brother offended is harder to be won than a strong city" (Proverbs 18:19).

THE SETTING SUN REACHED OUT, making a long shadow with
the eastbound bus. At the same time, the hills and mesas surrendered
to the open country of eastern New Mexico. Kee traveled with his face
glued to the window, his eyes straining to catch each change in the landscape in an attempt to make a mental map for a return trip. But it was a
losing battle. An air of hopeless resignation rose within him. He was feeling again. The memories of the day before stirred within him now. The
thought of losing his family, his friends, and the beloved mesas uncovered
the ache in his heart and, despite his effort to hold them back, tears began
their own journey down his face.

Within the roar of the bus's engine he fought for composure. Even as
the humming wheels took him further away by the second, Kee knew he
must find a way to be strong. As he reflected about his family in the middle of his loneliest moments, his thoughts shifted to Grandpa.

"Grandpa was already here!" he remembered. It was such a comforting
thought! "Grandpa was in Oklahoma. He made it back, and I am following his trail!" Kee suddenly knew that somehow he was going to make it.
No matter how bad it was, Grandpa had made it home, and he would, too!

As a big moon came up, Kee looked to the east and remembered the
story of the Navajo twins. They had gone east! It was there that they had
found their dad and received the lightning arrows. Maybe he, too, would

51

find his power in the east. Thoughts of his real dad were comforting and hopeful, though he doubted he'd find his dad in Oklahoma. No, his dad was a great medicine man whom he had never seen. Medicine men lived and worked among the Navajo people. Kee often fantasized about meeting his dad. He pictured himself to be tall and strong enough to make his dad like him and want to be with him. He already felt strong. Had he not stood up to the teacher and many students who had tried to shame him?

As the bus rushed on, Kee went back in his memories to other experiences that proved he was strong. He pictured every one of his victorious fights, and suddenly a memory that he had completely blocked out came back.

It was a forgotten episode with the skinwalker. He'd almost forgotten the time that he had been left alone with his baby brother while the others went to a neighbors' hogan for alcohol. It was at the time when Kee was still enjoying the freedom he had known before being hog-tied and sent to Chinle. Mother didn't approve, so he tried hard to win her back by doing extra chores. It was then that he had also fallen into looking after baby brother. Mother seemed to want and appreciate this, and Kee cared little for the wild times at the neighbors'—they were too crazy and frightening for him.

The sunset over the nearly desolate sheep camp prompted Kee to close the door of the hogan early. Little brother fell asleep after his bottle of powdered milk, and Kee remained awake, tending the fire in the little stove.

As he continued to gaze into the fire, he heard the chilling call: "Yi-yi-yi-yi-yi-yi!"

Kee's blood froze. His heart paused, then began to pound wildly as an old, sickening fear tried to smother him. The dogs barked frantically at first, then stopped and slunk away. Kee got up to inspect the bolt and peer through a crack in the door. He could see an erect figure behind a low bush near the hogan. Kee felt anger rise within him. It fought back his fear. He had heard his grandma say that he was more powerful than the skinwalker's curse, and now, alone, he felt he must stand up to the evil thing. But how should he do it? He remembered Grandpa saying, "You don't let da skinwalker tink you are afraid of it. If you are brave, it will be afraid of you!"

Grasping the bolt, Kee lifted it and cracked the door open.

The figure was that of a man who was covered with fur on the top part of his body. Large coyote ears rose from the back of his head, and he peered out from under the shade of the muzzle. He was a bit surprised that the door was opening and could not tell who was watching from the crack.

Kee held the door in position with one hand and grabbed an empty Coke bottle with the other. In one fluid motion he opened the door a little more and threw the bottle with all his strength. It was high of its mark, but it whistled loudly as it passed over the skinwalker's head.

Disappointed by the unexpected resistance, the evil thing lowered itself out of sight behind the bush. Kee felt no compulsion to investigate further. He bolted the door and checked on his sleeping brother before lying down and listening to the silence. The normal sounds of night returned before he could relax into a dreamless sleep. In the morning, after noting that the dogs were behaving normally, he walked out to the bush and checked for tracks. The fine sand showed no sign of human disturbance. Since little brother was still asleep, Kee walked around the entire camp but found no trace of the visitor.

The supernatural being (for that is what it was) is often confused with the regular skinwalkers, who are human agents doing damage on behalf of the dark side. But this spirit had come to draw Kee into his circle and there enslave him. It hadn't worked. Despite Kee's resentments and vulnerability, grace and love still had a place in his heart, and darkness could not yet overcome him.

The boy had planned to tell the others of the experience, but they had arrived in a collectively foul mood. Everyone was either hung over or bruised from the previous night, and Kee was put to work attending to an uncle who needed to have his hand wrapped after a punishing fist fight. Thus, the victorious and traumatic memory was lost in the shuffle of his attempts to find a place in the dysfunctional system.

The memory served Kee well. It bolstered his confidence as he rode on and on into the night on the eastbound bus, reflecting on the long-lost memory and its meaning. He would need the same courage again very soon.

When Kee reached the Oklahoma Indian school he found the structures and format to be very similar to what he had grown accustomed to in Chinle. Unfortunately, it gave him a sense of familiarity that caused him to relax his guard. Children from numerous tribes attended this school, and each tribe had formed gangs for their own protection and aggression. Some tribes had been bitter enemies throughout history and actually enjoyed a better relationship with the Anglo people than they did with each other. But since they were all "Indians," they were brought to this central staging ground to be properly educated.

After being shown his room, Kee was introduced to a couple of Navajo boys who had come from the New Mexico side of the reservation. Martin was short and chunky, and Emerson was taller than Kee and quite wiry.

Then Kee was allowed to roam the grounds before the next meal. Many children were in the playground area, and it was frightening to think of entering it without any friends to accompany him. So he began a stroll around the perimeter of the buildings to see what he could discover. Almost immediately he came upon a group of boys huddled around the side of the gymnasium, sharing a cigarette. One of the boys uttered a single word, and the others suddenly turned and pounced on Kee. Many hands grabbed and held him, while others began beating him unmercifully. Kee struggled to free himself, but it seemed hopeless.

Just as he began to feel himself going senseless from the pain, he heard a shout and saw a single figure breaking through the ring on his left. The tall person landed several hard blows on Kee's attackers, and soon they were all running. Kee staggered backward and bumped into the wall of the gym. When his vision cleared, he saw Emerson. "You OK?" he asked softly.

"Yes."

"Doze were Comanches," Emerson stated. "You gotta watch out for dem. If you stick around wid us Navajos you'll be OK. We help each other."

"OK," Kee said, nursing his bloody nose.

Emerson led him to the nursing station where he was scolded by a large Anglo nurse for getting into a fight. It was a harsh introduction but one that Kee would never forget. The trusting child within him became more watchful and suspicious.

But the experience had formed a bond between himself and Emerson. It was a bond with its own special brand of dysfunction. On one hand, Emerson protected him from attacks and introduced him to all the other

Navajos; but on the other, Emerson was a young addict, ready to medicate whenever he could.

A few days later a science teacher was leading a group of students through the back 40 acres to see a special wonder of nature. Emerson and Kee were trailing the others in the group when they noticed something off to one side. It was a curious-looking pile of dry sticks and branches. Within it they found a six-pack of beer, probably another student's stash. While the rest of the group followed the teacher farther into the trees, Emerson quickly downed two of the beers and offered one to Kee, who accepted. The boys then moved the remaining beer to a more secure location and covered them again before rejoining the science group.

The new location of the stash became a regular meeting place as six-pack replaced six-pack. Emerson, who was the size of a man, usually had little trouble getting the alcohol. He and Kee worked in the yards of the staff members or painted their fences to finance the purchases of alcohol in the nearby town. Kee developed a taste not only for the alcohol, but for the effect it had on his emotions. Many fits of laughter followed his drinking bouts with Emerson. Kee never knew he could have done so without the chemical that was beginning to dominate his conscious life.

On one field trip the students were allowed a little free time to shop. The two boys approached a bar, and Emerson took out a charcoal art pencil and darkened his mustache. "Here," he directed. "Go ahead; it'll make you look older too."

Kee took the pencil and copied Emerson's strokes before giving it back and following his friend into the bar. The darkness was frightening at first, but as the boys settled on their stools they appreciated the concealment it afforded. It was Kee's first time in a bar, and as is often the case, it passed in a seemingly harmless manner. After a couple of beers, the boys headed out to rejoin their group. Much later, Kee would learn more of the devastating effects that come while drinking in a bar.

School was not difficult for Kee, at least when he was sober and not preoccupied with thoughts of his home, family, and friends. His grades were above average, and the teachers thought him a promising prospect. Kee, however, had no intention of taking on their values, and he had little trust left for anyone in the governmental system. He found out when the first break would be and kept that date, like a treasure, in his mind. It was his motivation. When he had first arrived in Oklahoma he'd been told that if he failed here there were other schools, even further from Navajoland, to which he could be sent. It was warning enough for him.

The first school break came, and Kee could hardly believe it when the bus started taking him west. It couldn't go fast enough! But the vacation did accelerate after he arrived back at his mesa. Ironically, while nothing had changed, Kee realized that *he* had changed. There was a restlessness that he couldn't understand. His family greeted him warmly and commented on how tall he had gotten, but Kee needed more. In the morning he jogged up the mesa and hiked to the spring. Its waters were still sweet and cool. The scent of the juniper and grasses filled him with a nostalgic feeling that was comforting. Then his mind went to the cigarettes in his travel bag, and a craving shot into his body.

The break went well enough. Grandpa tried to remind him to stay out of fights, and showed him the garden. Grandma made him lots of frybread. Little brother had to show him all his toys, and Mother showed him the new rug she was weaving. Her man was gone, and Kee didn't want to inquire about him. It would be rude to do so.

Strangely enough, the person he enjoyed the most was his great-auntie Mary. He made more than one trip over the hill and behind the rocks to her hogan. She was without a man but not without her bottles of "medicine." So Kee sat down on that old bench, his long legs stretched out to the place he had once stood in childhood to have his first drink. But it didn't matter to him anymore. He was glad to have someone to share laughter and alcohol with, and so was Auntie.

Kee was amazed at the speed with which the break time passed, but he was able to pull himself away without too much effort. He remembered his buddy, Emerson, and that was enough to help him get back on the bus.

So the cycle completed itself again and again: trips to the Oklahoma school, secret alcohol binges, a return to the mesa, and parties with Auntie. It was a wonder that Kee was able to keep his grades up to the average level for as long as he did. It couldn't last forever, though, and when it came crashing down he shouldn't have been surprised.

It started at a drinking party with some of his buddies in the dormitory. They had secretly been bringing bottles of beer into their living quarters for some time, but one of the children had finally blown the whistle on them, and the dean had come to break it up. Unfortunately, Emerson was too drunk to think clearly. When the dean tried to grab the drink out of his hand, Emerson struck the dean in the face and knocked him over. Stunned, the dean crawled away and stumbled off to call the sheriff. The other boys became frightened and left, but Kee sat by his friend and tried to calm him.

It was the first time Kee had seen him so unreasonable. Emerson continued drinking until five sheriffs arrived. When they surrounded him, he suddenly stood up and decked the officer in front of him with one hard blow. The other four officers were on him immediately, but another one was knocked down as well. Kee knew it was futile to join the fight, but after the remaining three sheriffs wrestled Emerson to the ground, handcuffed him, and began beating him with billy clubs, Kee lost control. Jumping to his feet he yelled, "Stop!" and tackled the nearest officer. The two rolled about on the floor, which caused the other two officers to cease their punishment of Emerson. Suddenly they were all over Kee, and in moments they had him pinned and handcuffed.

A crowd of big boys had gathered, and the officers didn't want anyone else jumping them. So Kee was spared the blows that Emerson had taken. The officers asked the dean who else had been involved in the drinking. With his help they found the other boys and took them out to their cars, along with Emerson and Kee.

It was Kee's first night in jail. However, with all his drinking buddies to keep him company, the large room with bars on the windows wasn't so bad. The following day they were brought before a judge, who released all of them except Kee and Emerson. When the principal visited him that afternoon, Kee was told he would be shipped to the Phoenix Indian School. It took another night and day in the jail before all the arrangements could be made, and Kee remained in confinement until he was released and put on the bus.

Emerson hadn't been seen since the first morning when they had gone before the judge, but one of the officers told Kee about his sentence: three months in the county jail.

Kee boarded the bus without protest. His heart was torn over

Emerson's situation, but he was heading closer to Navajoland. The "hot place" would be tough for him, but he would be ready this time.

As the bus followed the winding highway down into the desert, Kee reflected on what he had learned thus far. Grandpa was right—he should never trust Bilagaanas. He now identified with the renegades of the past. He was a young warrior and proud of it! His people had only lost to Kit Carson because they didn't have weapons of equal efficiency. He knew it was futile to fight against so many people, but he would never give in to them, either. He would learn all their ways, and he would not let them outsmart him.

The large and bewildering Phoenix bus depot was his first challenge, yet Kee managed to keep his sullen mood. He wouldn't let anyone know he was afraid.

"Kee Nez?" a pleasant-looking, browned-skinned man asked.

Kee nodded. He was actually relieved to see the man, even though it meant another trip to an Indian school.

"Welcome to Phoenix! I'm Mr. Martinez, the history teacher."

Kee only shrugged and stared blankly at the man. Inwardly, the man had already made a good impression, but Kee was determined not to like him. He had experienced too many letdowns with teachers before.

"My car is right over this way." The man gestured with his head, almost in the Navajo way of pointing with the lips, Kee thought as he followed the man. Maybe he was some other kind of Indian.

It was a hot spring afternoon, and the teacher's car was not equipped with air-conditioning. Kee rolled down his window but found little comfort in the hot air blowing in the window. He endured it for a few minutes before rolling it up again.

Mr. Martinez noticed and pulled into a grocery store. "The best way to beat the heat is to get something nice and cold to drink," he said as he opened his door. "Come on; let's get a soda."

Kee was not used to such friendly gestures from Indian school staff and didn't budge. The teacher looked at him once through the windshield then headed inside. He knew that the sun would make Kee sorry soon enough, but he was also afraid that Kee might bolt for the street, so he hurriedly paid for two Cokes and returned to the car. Kee hadn't moved an inch, but he did manage to wordlessly receive the soda when it was offered.

The Indian school in Phoenix had the usual drab buildings, but the grounds were dotted with flowers and waving palm trees, which were new to Kee. Within his gloomy heart a spark of hope that this place would be better than the others began to glow like an ember in Grandma's stove. Mr. Martinez didn't immediately take him to the dormitory. He gave him a tour of the grounds and made a special point to show him where his office was.

"Anytime you need something, come by," he offered. "I'll do what I can to help you."

Kee made no response. He was surprised by Mr. Martinez and didn't know what to say. Part of him wanted to tell the teacher that he would never be coming by for any reason, but another part felt comforted by the genuine offer.

When they got to the dorm, Kee was introduced to the dean and other boys in his vicinity. It was all so familiar now, and he began looking for someone he could relate to. Most of the boys were shorter and stockier than Kee, and he guessed that they might be Pima.

That evening in the cafeteria he noticed some Navajo boys. They were lankier than he, and had classic Athabaskan features. After the meal was over he visited with them and found out that they were from the New Mexico side of the reservation. One was even related to Emerson. Kee told them what had happened to his friend and how he came to be transferred to Phoenix. The boys immediately welcomed him into their circle. They had a common bond, and it was understood without many words.

The next morning in class Kee's sullen mood had taken over again. The gloom of his situation and the smoldering anger that comes from long-ignored wishes were building within him. He wanted a smoke or a drink—anything to give vent to his emotions.

By early afternoon the temperature was more than 100° F and still climbing. Kee's mental state wasn't improving, though. After lunch the boys had a free period out on the playground. A short, stocky boy with muscular limbs sat in the shade and made a comment about Kee's height as he passed by. Kee stopped and turned his withering gaze at the boy, who stood up quickly. It was clear that he had an attitude, too. The two boys took steps toward each other, each with their own vendetta against the world.

"Kee! Jackson!" called a strong but friendly voice. "Here!"

It was Mr. Martinez, who had just emerged from the cafeteria. His clear call made both boys pause and look at him. Seizing the momentum, the teacher quickly strode over to them. Both boys glared at him then back at each other.

He was moving between them now. His expression was serious. "I want both of you to come to my office," he said. "Come on!"

They followed, somewhat relieved at having a face-saving way to avoid the fight. Each had second thoughts about his own ability to beat the other. Now the pre-fight tension gave way to wonder about the consequences that awaited them in the office.

Once inside the small room the teacher went to a little refrigerator and got out two bottles of soda. He gave one to each of the boys and asked them to sit down. The boys complied, and Mr. Martinez went into a lecture on the "good life," beginning with the story of how he, as a child, came to an Indian school and got into a fight with another boy, who later became his best friend. He told about his journey to wholeness and happiness through a spiritual experience with the Creator.

Both boys listened as they sipped on their sodas. When their drinks were finished, so also was Mr. Martinez's story. They all stood, and he asked the boys to shake hands and make peace.

After a moment's hesitation, the shorter boy extended his hand and Kee briefly took it in a gentle shake. He was grateful for the drink and the story. He had never heard anything like it before. It gave him a hopeful hint that perhaps even the tangled mess of his own childhood could be used for some greater purpose.

Later that afternoon he sat in Mr. Martinez's American history class. He was discussing the period of the late 1800s, and talking about Natives being forced to move onto reservations. Kee learned many things that day not only about other tribes, but also about some good White people who had lobbied hard for fairness and the honoring of treaties. Kee did not know that such people had ever existed. It gave an indirect challenge to his own racial bias.

As the days and weeks passed, Kee made many trips to Mr. Martinez's office, sometimes because the teacher sensed he needed the attention and invited him, and other times because Kee just decided to drop in. The little refrigerator never ran out of sodas, and the man never ran out of patience. He talked to Kee about how wonderful it would be to graduate from high school, and what great things he could do with his life, as well as many other encouraging ideas.

Gradually, Kee began to buy into some of the ideas, and by the time summer vacation rolled around, he was sure he wanted to come back in the fall. The spark of hope had fanned itself into a little flame that now burned in the center of his soul.

Two years later, without any active drug habits, he graduated at the top of his class. The Phoenix gymnasium was packed with people from many tribes. However, even though Kee had invited them, none of his relatives attended. Many were without transportation of their own, but Kee knew that sometimes they had gone on bus trips to other events. Mr. Martinez and his wife were there, and they had a special card and gift for him.

Kee left the school with a suitcase that Mr. and Mrs. Martinez had given him and a myriad of educational memories. He paused only once to turn and wave to Mr. Martinez. He couldn't know that he would never see the man again. The world was his to explore, yet his first wish was to return to his beloved mesa.

CHAPTER 8

Disillusioned Wanderings

"Let the wicked forsake his way, and the unrighteous man his thoughts"
(Isaiah 55:7).

I T WAS THE SORT OF GENTLE afternoon that almost compensated Kee for earlier insanties of his life, pushing them deeper into his subconscious. The friendly sun of early summer warmed the red rocks on the top of the Utah mesa just enough to make him feel sleepy as he lay on them, scanning the valley floor. A soft breeze stirred him with its freshness before it danced away, taking with it all memory of the noise of Phoenix. He was finally free from school, but deep within him lurked an uneasiness that kept him from pure joy.

From his vantage point he could see the sheep camp and Grandma's and Mother's hogans. He could even see the tiny figure of Grandpa down in a draw with the sheep, some three miles away. It looked like a barren land, but the sheep were good at locating the tufts of grass that dug their roots stubbornly into the sides of the ravines and gullies. Kee could almost hear the sheep as they nipped and nibbled their way along. The sound of their plucking and chewing was one of his earliest memories.

His eyes darted to the left, focusing on Aunt Mary's hogan beyond the rocks. She sat in a chair just outside the only door. He knew she was drunk. Auntie Mary was always moving from one level of intoxication to another. Whether it was home brew or alcohol from a bootlegger, she always found a way to get alcohol. What made matters worse was the fact that Joe, the most prominent bootlegger in the area, was her new boyfriend. The pretty blue pickup was missing, so he must be gone. It didn't make a difference to Kee; he had stopped drinking several months before graduating at the Indian school and wanted to keep it that way. That was why he had been avoiding Aunt Mary since his return from school. All the same, he did admire her new boyfriend's pickup. He knew it had been purchased with bootlegging money, and he'd also noticed that bootleggers seemed to do better financially than his relatives.

It had been a quiet homecoming; nothing more than the usual smiles and handshakes. But it was enough for Kee. Graduation was not a great milestone in his family's reckoning. Even though he was the first one ever to have graduated from high school, he understood there were other priorities. It was enough to be alive and to be there for your relatives when they needed you.

The problem was he was getting tired of the *way* his relatives needed him. The helping out with work was not a problem, but breaking up the frequent drunken fights and watching the whole "binge cycle" again and again was starting to get to him.

Kee shifted his gaze back to Grandpa. From this distance his tiny figure among the white specks of sheep stirred a fondness in his heart that brought him closer to tears than he had been in a long while. He remembered the old man's words from the night before.

"Da day after tomorrow I go to Gallup, and you can come too!"

The old man stood now, shimmery in the waves of heat. The sun's brightness was hard to ignore. Kee glanced upward at the intense light, and it triggered within him a more distant flashback. When he was about 9, he had asked his mother a question, and he suddenly recalled the entire conversation.

"My mother, at the squaw dance I heard the medicine men talking about somebody," he began. "They said, 'Because he came, it is beautiful.' Who were they talking about? Who made it beautiful?"

"It's the sun," she had stated, "the dad of the twin heroes."

He had accepted her answer simply, but now he questioned it. He questioned many things these days. Mother's answer no longer made sense. The sun dried up everything and made things barren and ugly late in the summer. The twins' dad seemed to be someone interested only in his own well being. He had not helped the twins' mom—he had left her, behaving in the same way that his own dad had behaved. Kee had never received any help from his dad. No; the rocks, earth, and sky were beautiful without the sun's help. He knew *someone* had done it, but still wondered who had come to make it beautiful. Maybe it was the God that the Bilagaana told about. That One sounded more like He was nice.

The sun seemed to sense Kee's thoughts and turned up the temperature, making him uncomfortable in the heat. He rose to his feet and stretched with a yawn. The trail to the bottom was well known, and he hardly noticed it as he thought again of going to Gallup. He knew the veterans' office and hospital where Grandpa would go to get help with the required paperwork or occasional treatments. A new plan was formulating in his mind. For a number of months Kee had been thinking about joining the army. There was a fight going on in a place called Vietnam, and it was honorable to be a warrior. He decided, as he went down the trail, that he would enlist when he went with Grandpa to Gallup. He had been home from school for only a short time and, ironically, needed some new adventure to occupy his mind, a new direction to escape being with his beloved family for too long! His beautiful mesa and surrounding country were too familiar now. Besides the location of the skinwalker cave, there was nothing else to discover, and that place seemed worse than war.

Kee didn't tell anyone about his plan as he settled in for the night. He didn't want anyone to try and stop him. Besides, he had not felt free to share his inner feelings and dreams with anyone for a very long time. The hogan was crowded with his little brother and Mother's new man. It would probably be better for everyone if he left.

The next morning the relative's old pickup rattled into the camp before the sun was up. Kee wondered if the old machine would make it all the way to Gallup, but that was only one of many uncertainties that attended many reservation events: "Will the truck make it to town?" "Will there be enough food for everyone?" "How will we reach them without a phone?" "How will we get the money for this?" "Who knows how to fix that?" The problems and perplexities were so common, and the emotions attached to them were often unexpressed.

The spotted and rusty pickup did manage to rumble into Gallup. As usual, Indian Town U.S.A., as it is sometimes called, was a beehive of activity that afternoon. It welcomed Apaches from the east and west, the Hopi people from the northwest, the Zuni from the south, Navajos from the east, north, and west, and other Pueblo tribes from the east. Its citizens were as mixed as its visitors. But while some tolerated Natives for the sake of business, others despised the situation and looked for reasons to discriminate. Kee, however, didn't learn of this until much later.

He went with Grandpa to the veteran's office first and straightened out Grandpa's paperwork with the government. Then they went to the trading post of the "yelling man." That wasn't the owner's real name. The Navajos had their own names for most of the Anglo people they had dealings with, usually connected with some facet of their character. Kee remembered the Mormon trader farther north who was called "red devil." It made him wonder whether he should do any major trading with that man. But Grandpa wanted to go to the yelling man's place because the trader had something that Grandma had told him she wanted.

After Grandpa made the purchase, they walked to the nearest bar. Grandpa went in, and Kee headed for the recruiting office a few blocks away. While most of the young men of the country were trying to avoid the draft in those days, many of the Natives were looking for employment—and success—through the military. Kee's heritage lent itself well to the futile struggle in Vietnam. Many Native Americans would die on that foreign soil.

Once in the office, Kee quickly signed up and was moved to the physical examination room where he slipped to the end of the check-up line as the doctor was making a check of earlier applicants. He removed his shirt as he was instructed and awaited his turn. It was an awkward time for the modest young man.

"Kee Nez," the doctor called gruffly. "Stand over here."

Kee complied with each of the doctor's orders. He squatted low on his knees to show their health, opened his mouth wide for the oral exam, and held still while the doctor listened with the stethoscope to his chest.

"Young man," the doctor said gravely, "you have a heart murmur. The armed forces cannot accept anyone with a heart murmur!"

Kee was stunned. He wasn't sure what a heart murmur was, but he was very clear on the part about not being accepted. "But—I'm strong! I run up the mesa without stopping!"

"That may be," said the doctor wryly, "but the Army won't take you."

Kee was crushed. Since childhood he had thought about being a warrior like Grandpa, and now this strange man was telling him that he was rejected from his dream. He was too upset to speak as he put his shirt back on and stormed out of the office. It was a shame and dishonor that he hardly knew how to handle. It reminded him of the principal in Oklahoma who had shipped him off to Phoenix.

He found Grandpa in the bar, sitting on a stool, chatting with a couple of old acquaintances. They were there on business of their own from the same part of the reservation.

"Hey, sonny!" Grandpa was in a happy mood. "You gonna drink with me now?"

"My grandpa," Kee said cooly, "our relative is waiting with the truck. It's the time that we said we would be there."

"OK, sonny." Grandpa's mood was unaffected. "Let's go!"

All the way home Grandpa sang and talked about his summer plans. He was going to work in the Idaho potato fields, and then he was going to pick pinion pine nuts. At one point he invited Kee to join him, and this seemed to comfort Kee a bit. His pain and shame over the military rejection would affect him for years, but he was grateful to have an option that involved something besides staying home.

The old pickup made it back to camp with only one small problem when it tried to cross the sandy wash. But Kee and Grandpa managed to push it out of the rut, and now they were talking to the owner about a ride to the Flagstaff bus station in a few days. The time was established, and the driver was paid for his gas before the last light of sunset was gone from the sky.

Kee silently took his disappointment to bed with him. The hurt in his heart added to the uneasiness about the murmur. What was a murmur? He concluded that it couldn't be too important if he could run and ride with ease. Probably it was just one of those silly Anglo things, like test scores when the teacher had given the last A to the student with the score only one point higher than his.

Idaho was an adventure that soon wore itself out. Kee was pleased to see the beauty of the new country, but the rising temperature and repetitious work with a hoe in the field became old quickly. He liked the pay and the chance to buy whatever he wanted, but mostly he was inclined to save his money for something bigger. Grandpa was good company, and the laughter helped compensate for some of the monotony in the fields.

The season ended none too soon. Kee had learned how much the farmer was making for the potatoes he was harvesting, and the dollar figure made him jealous. He was ready to return to the land of the Navajo. He had discovered that there are some things more boring than staying at home. For his part, Grandpa was expecting that the money he'd made would add to the popularity he still hoped to have with Grandma. The relationship was formal, at best, but the old man wanted to be in good with the older woman. He had nowhere else to go, and truly had a hidden fondness for her.

The bus trip home was more enjoyable than the trip to Idaho had been because both of them had money to spend on the way. Once in Flagstaff, they were able to catch a ride in the back of a pickup heading into Navajoland. It got them to Tuba City, where they again hitched a ride to Monument Valley. They walked the last few miles with grateful hearts. It had been a long summer, and they were enjoying the sights and smells of the land.

The temperature around the mesa remained warm during the day, dropping at night. It happened every year around October, when the snakes crawled down into their caves and holes to spend another winter in their coils. The pinion pine trees also changed by allowing the cold of the night to pop their pine cones open and expose their nuts before dropping them. The Navajos looked for the places where these trees were yielding their nuts and harvested them for a special staple during the cold season. The trading posts had also found a way to make money on these tasty little nuts. Sometimes they would buy from the Navajos, later selling them back at a higher price. Other times they would ship them off to far away places, where they were considered a special delicacy. Either way, Grandpa always went looking for them, and this year Kee would not have school to keep him away from the outing.

They had heard that the San Fransico Peaks were loaded with pinions that year, but before they could go the matter of firewood had to be attended to. So Kee made a number of trips up the mesa to replenish the wood stack between Mother's and Grandma's hogans, while Grandpa gave Grandma a break from the sheep.

The old spotted pickup was down for repairs, so Auntie Mary's boot-legger boyfriend was approached for a ride to the Flagstaff area. The man made many runs to Flagstaff and Winslow to buy beer from the Bilagaanas, so it was no problem for him. This way the trip would pay both ways!

Kee enjoyed riding in the shiny blue pickup. The owner was obviously a very successful Navajo, and Kee couldn't help admiring him. An undetected seed of envy was planted in his heart that day. If only he could enjoy such a nice vehicle . . . But there were few jobs on the reservation, other than the usual tribal and federal government jobs that often required higher education.

Once in the pines, Kee forgot his wishes and got into the timeless beauty of the mountains. San Francisco Peaks are one of the four sacred mountains of the Navajo people. Some said that there were spirits living in these mountains, and anyone living within the perimeter of them would have a good life. Kee felt the goodness of his life in that place. The pinions were plentiful and large, and it took only a few days until they had many pounds of them.

During this time Kee experienced something with his grandpa that made a lasting impression. They were picking nuts with other Navajos one evening when a distraught mother came crying to them. She had not seen her son for several hours, and it was getting dark. After describing the boy to them, she rushed into the woods, calling his name as she went. Grandpa watched the woman go, then turned and headed in the opposite direction and climbed a small hill. Kee followed, wondering what he would do.

Once on the hilltop, Grandpa began a chant and held his right hand out in front of him. As he chanted, the hand began to tremble. The shaking increased, and Kee was frightened as he watched. It appeared that Grandpa had lost control of his hand, and someone else was jiggling it. The old man's hand moved in different directions as it shook. Kee was wondering if he should do something to help his grandpa when it finally stopped.

"Come!" Grandpa ordered. "Da boy is ober dare!" He pointed with his chin in the last direction in which his shaking hand had pointed.

Without another word the two set off in the direction indicated by Grandpa. Within minutes they had located the boy and were heading back to the camping area with him. The mother was overjoyed later that evening when she was reunited with her son, and Kee had a new respect for his grandpa.

A few days later they were breaking camp and lugging burlap sacks full of nuts. The total amount was nearly 100 pounds. The duo managed to hitch a ride with one of the other nut gatherers, and reached the sheep camp none too soon. Strong winds had arrived early, bringing the early snow storms behind them. The intensity of the storms and the amount of snow they delivered were something Kee didn't remember witnessing before.

On the morning after their arrival Kee woke up to the sound of Mother struggling with the door. Her new man was gone, and the heavy snowdrift outside made it impossible to get out. Quickly Kee jumped to his feet and joined his mother in the struggle. Soon the door was open enough for Kee to squeeze through. He floundered in the three-foot snowbank, trying to locate an old shovel on the side of the hogan. He then dug out the doorway and blazed a trail to the woodpile.

Down by the sheep corral Kee noticed a new, white mound by the fence. He dug a trail in that direction, and on closer inspection discovered a stack of hay. Grandma must have taken the wagon to the trading post two days before and pawned her silver necklace, rings, and bracelets for the hay. Kee shoveled over to her hogan and dug her door out. She greeted him with a smile once she could open the door. He remarked about the hay, and her smile grew broader.

"Da wind and da birds, day told me!" she exclaimed.

The rest of the day passed with short trips to the wood pile, outhouse, and sheep corral. They started roasting and enjoying the pinions that they had intended to sell in Gallup. As it turned out, the pinions were an important part of their survival that long winter. As the weeks went by and the snow continued to accumulate, the staples were used up, one by one, and the family's diet dwindled to mutton stew and pinions.

Kee often did the butchering so that the older ones didn't have to strain themselves in the chilling drifts. Often, after going through the effort of roping the chosen sheep and wrestling it to the ground to tie its feet together, he would slit its throat and quickly open its belly so that he could plunge his hands in among the entrails to warm up. It was just a fact of life, almost as normal as breathing.

The family became concerned when the pile of hay began to shrink and the woodpile got low. Kee took the shovel and struggled to blaze a trail up the mesa where he knew he could find more firewood. His people never took a living tree for fuel. They would look at a forest of trees and say, "Dare's no wood around here!" But Kee knew where the dead snags were located, and he persisted until he reached that part of the mesa.

Once the fuel problem was solved, everyone's concern focused on the sheep. The snow was too deep for them to reach the little tufts of grass that usually sustained them, and no one could go out far enough to bring back hay for them. The herd was reduced because of the heavy diet of mutton, and the thought of losing the entire herd to starvation was very troubling to the older ones in the family.

Kee's childlike qualities seemed to come out more with the snow. He looked at every problem as a challenging game. He had solved the firewood problem, and now he was celebrating his new trail up the mesa by dragging the hood of an old car up the slope with some rope, then sliding down the side of the mesa in it. The hay didn't concern him so much because he knew there was still about a two day's supply left. Who knew what might happen before the last day of the haystack arrived? In the meantime, his dishlike toboggan provided great entertainment.

The trip up the mesa with the car hood was as slow and boring as the trip down was fast and frightening. More than once Kee ended up in a heap in the deep snow, while the car hood shot on down the steep slope, bouncing and flipping.

It was on one of his tedious return trips up the mesa that he heard a strange sound, a sound he'd once heard in Phoenix, though at first he couldn't place it. He recognized it in the same moment that the helicopter rounded the side of the mesa. From his prominent position, Kee let go of the rope and began waving wildly. The car hood made a quick escape down the side of the mesa as the helicopter veered closer. Someone inside waved, while Kee pointed down at the sheep camp. The helicopter lowered itself toward the camp, and acknowledged the figures that had appeared out of the hogans and were gesturing toward the sheep corral.

The helicopter hovered for a few more moments then disappeared around the side of the mesa that it had yet to explore. Kee felt encouraged and disappointed at the same time. Did they understand their situation?

Why hadn't they been helped? He slipped and stumbled his way down the mesa to see what the others thought.

The next day Kee heard the sound again, and this time the chopper came directly to the camp. It hovered over by the sheep corral then dropped several bales of hay. Everyone cheered and waved their thanks. The new tribal chairman was doing a good job of getting help for his people!

Soon the warmer air won its yearly battle with the north wind, and before the chopper could make its fourth hay drop, the sheep were out nibbling in the wash again. It had been a long winter for the young warrior, and while he was glad to have been home to help his family, the monotony of the weeks had taken their toll. Kee had a new plan and enough unspent money to make it happen.

One early spring morning he walked out to where Grandpa was herding the sheep. It was a private spot, away from the rest of the family.

"My grandpa," Kee began, "I think I want to go work on the railroad like you did, but I don't know where to go."

"Dat's OK, sonny!" the old man said. "I took a bus to dat big town, Denber, and at da train station der, day gabe me da job. Den I went on a train to Wyomeen. It's a big trip!"

"Thank you, my grandpa. I think I'll be going there."

"Good!" the old shepherd said, and turned back to watch his flock. He knew there was no stopping Kee. He was a young man, and an elder's advice is often wasted. He had lived long enough to know that no matter how far in the world a restless heart may wander, it always seeks to return to rest between the four sacred mountains.

Kee was not thinking about this as he gathered his few belongings in an old military backpack and said farewell to the rest of his family. Strangely enough, it was his little brother, Johnson, whom he found the hardest to leave. Over the winter Johnson had become a little buddy and had provided hours of diversion. Kee, on the other hand, was Johnson's hero, who had gone off on great adventures and always came back with little treats for him. Johnson tried not to cry, but as Kee headed out the door he heard the little boy's sob, and the sound struck deeply in his heart. He turned around and rushed back in to his brother. Down on one knee, he looked in the child's eyes and explained that he had to go in order to get him another surprise.

Once outside, the picture of his brother's tear-brimmed eyes haunted him. It was a reflection of his own wounded child, abandoned long ago by many—even by himself. Kee couldn't consciously put it together at the time, but it gnawed at him all the same.

He had little trouble hitching a ride to Flagstaff; then he caught a bus to Denver. The Mile High City was a frighteningly confusing place, but a taxi driver helped him locate the train station—and took most of his remaining cash. Jobs were plentiful, especially since Vietnam was taking so many young men away. Kee was signed on with the railroad in a matter of hours after arriving in Denver, and the next day he was taking his first ride on the rails to western Nebraska.

The new crew was a multiethnic group comprised mainly of Mexicans, Navajos, African-Americans, Irish, Swedes, and men of Slavic descent. On the way to the job site the new crew members stored their items in one general area. At lunch time one of the African-Americans accidentally picked the wrong lunch sack. He discovered this when he reached in and felt a small, clay-covered figure in the sack. Curious, he tried to take it out of the sack, and broke it open to find the bone and flesh of a prairie dog.

"Yuck! What is this?" he exclaimed. "There's a dead animal in this sack!"

One of the Navajos hurried over to claim his special meal, a delicacy from home that he had saved for this part of the trip. The other men wanted to know what the uproar was about, but it took several minutes to explain, and by then everyone was laughing.

When Navajos succeed in killing a prairie dog, they have a special way of preparing it. After the unfortunate creature is gutted, its exterior is packed with clay, and it is buried in the sand. Then a fire is made over the burial spot, and hours later the prairie dog is dug up, cooked, and preserved inside the clay shell. Kee knew how much some of the older people liked prairie dog meat. He had killed a few, and it was one of the few times in his life that he had received passionate expressions of gratitude from his grandma. He now figured that this fellow railroad employee had a loving relative back home who had sent the special lunch along.

Kee's strength and size made him a natural on the railroad crew. The hard work of shoveling and lifting ties was a challenge he enjoyed. He had little interest in the bars that the men entered when they reached a town. The foreman noticed these qualities, and soon Kee was elevated to a higher paying position.

━ ━ ━

Spring passed, and summer began in earnest. The heat wave shortened tempers, and many a crew member came to blows with a fellow worker. Kee managed to avoid these brawls, partly because of his size, and partly because he had developed a sense for when trouble was brewing and would leave the area. It wasn't entertaining to watch a fight anymore. In fact, deep down, Kee knew he had never really liked it.

One sweltering July day Kee found himself in a situation that he no longer could avoid. His foreman's supervisor, who was visiting the work site, started chewing him out for something that had not been done properly. The foreman saw Kee standing nearby and wrongly blamed him for it. The supervisor then told the foreman to demote Kee, and it was done. This act of injustice grieved Kee. He knew he was innocent, and even though he could handle the new assignment, the dishonor prompted him to walk away from the railroad crew after his next paycheck. There were no words of explanation and no two-week notice, just a Navajo getting on the next bus for Flagstaff. When the foreman later checked his smaller crew and found Kee missing, he felt more justified in getting the jump on another "irresponsible" Indian.

Kee was lulled by the now familiar sound of the humming wheels of the big bus. The way his job had turned out seemed to match the story of his childhood education, and it burned him. Why go through the effort to work in the White man's world if it always had such an unsatisfying end? Before he hitched a ride out of Flagstaff, he stopped at the shopping center and bought a shiny red wagon for his little brother. It was something Kee had always wanted as a child, and he smiled, thinking about how much Johnson would enjoy it.

CHAPTER 9

In Search of Good Medicine

"And there appeared a great wonder in heaven; a woman clothed with the sun, and the moon under her feet" (Revelation 12:1).

THE LOUD CHANTING WAS MONOTONOUS. It didn't have the high intensity of the singers in the Peyote religion, in which the rapid drumbeats added to the mystical silhouettes on the canvas walls of the tepee. But Kee had little interest in joining those who ate of the Peyote medicine plant. He had tried it and found it lacking. No, this was a more familiar, even comforting, sort of chant from old men beating rawhide stretched over metal drums at the squaw dance.

Kee thought about the word "squaw." It wasn't a Navajo word. It wasn't even a nice word, yet his people used it for this type of gathering. He knew it was a dance where he could hold a woman's hand, but the thought terrified him. No one had ever taught him how to dance, and women could be intimidating.

In the evening light his eyes scanned the crowd, wondering if someone had seen the inner fear reflected in his face. On the opposite side of the shade house the firelight shone brightly in the eyes of a beautiful young woman. She was obviously watching him, and Kee could feel her attraction touching his heart like the gentle stroke of an eagle feather. It thrilled and frightened him at the same time.

He held her gaze for a moment before turning toward the fire where the food was being cooked. A few strides brought him nearer the heat, but he was already sweating as he got in line for a plate of food. It was a good diversion that bought him some time. Why was his heart pounding faster than the drums? He tried to understand what had come over him and told himself to calm down.

After enjoying several mouthfuls in a distant part of the gathering, he was beginning to feel more relaxed when he heard a soft woman's voice behind him.

"Here!" she said, and Kee twisted his head around to see a can of Pepsi being extended to him by a lovely brown hand. A simple silver bracelet graced her wrist, and as he turned to see more, his eyes followed the blue velvet sleeve back to the beautiful face.

"Thank you!" he said softly as he took the can. It was unopened, and he busied himself with putting his plate down and opening it. Picking up the plate again, he noticed from his peripheral vision that she was gone. He turned to look, but she had melted into the crowd.

Now Kee was curious—and worried. Who was this young woman? He had never seen her at the gatherings before. Why did she come, and then disappear? Had she lost her interest in him after a closer examination?

He finished his food in short order and threw the paper plate in the fire, then strolled about holding the soda can. The singers had paused, and people were milling about, but he couldn't spot the one person he was looking for.

The singers resumed with a song about "beauty." Kee, returning to the place where he had been sitting to eat his food, began tracking her footprints in the dust. His grandpa had taught him how to track years ago when they were looking for lost sheep. But now he was tracking a greater prize, and his heart wrenched with the empty desire. Those few moments when he was held in her eyes had been so wonderful—he wanted more! She couldn't have just disappeared . . . It all had been too real!

By the marks in the red dirt he could tell that she hadn't worn the traditional Navajo moccasins. He remembered she had on the decorative go-go boots of the 1960s, and now he had little trouble following her tracks out into the shadows beyond the firelight.

Once he had reached the outer ring of darkness beyond the fire, it became too dark to see the tracks. But he noticed that they were headed toward the wood pile, so he maintained that course. Laughter greeted him as he rounded the stack of wood.

"So you came to help me!" said a soft voice.

"Yes," Kee stated.

"OK, here." Kee suddenly felt an armload of wood being pressed into his chest. His arms instinctively responded, and in the process of taking the wood, he touched her hand. It was surprisingly soft, and he felt thrilled and embarrassed for noticing.

He turned and headed for the main fire, thankful for the darkness. He kept his head down as he reentered the firelight and busied himself with building up the flames. Back at the wood stack, he found her chopping in the moonlight. Navajo women are very good with an ax, and chopping wood was considered honorable women's work. She paused while he stooped to gather more wood from the ground. This time the wood exchange was a tenth of a second slower before he headed this time for the cooking fire and deposited a load there. She was still at the stack when he returned, and Kee was ready for a more direct approach.

"Where are you from?"

"I walk around Moon Water," she said, referring to her community.

"What is your clan?" Kee asked the question, fearing the worst. Among his people, the complicated clan system determined who your relatives were and whom you could marry. In the clan system a person whom you've never seen before could be considered your relative by mutual clan connections. Thus, some people cannot marry, because this is considered incestuous.

"Me? I'm from da water flowing people," she responded. "What about you?"

"Sleeping rock," he answered.

Both were relieved. A major taboo was not standing between them. Both smiled in the moonlight, and Kee suddenly realized how short she was. He could not hold himself back from a little tease. Everyone knew that the Hopis and Acomas tended to be shorter in stature. So he impulsively went for a verbal jab.

"I thought you might be from the Pueblo people because you're so tall!"

Even in the moonlight Kee could see her eyes flash. "I thought dat you might be from da pine tree people because you're so short!" Her quick reply and sharp tongue made him realize that she was not a person easily given to taking a joke.

He decided to try a different strategy. "Have you been to the top of my mesa over there?" He pointed with his lips toward the mesa about a mile away.

"No."

"It's pretty. I know the trail real well—even in the dark."

Her eyes widened. "You go up der in da dark?"

"Many times. I even sleep up there."

"Doesn't the skinwalker come and visit you?"

"Not anymore," Kee replied. "I think he got scared of me." Then Kee launched into the story of the time he threw the bottle at the evil being, and she listened to him with unabashed wonder in her eyes. Quite obviously she was terrified of the skinwalkers and was amazed by his courage and strength of will.

When he finished talking, it was her turn to share something that she had told only to her younger sister. For some reason, it was easy to talk with Kee, so she told of her own dreadful encounter.

"One day I was wid my mom's sheep, but I lef' for da camp too late in da afternoon. As I was coming home by da big rocks, dis skinwalker jumps up at me. I could tell it was a woman, and it had a wooden pipe in its mouth. Den, before I could do anything, it blew dis powder in my face, and it made me pass out. But my younger sister, she was worried about me, and I didn't know it but she was coming and calling for me when she saw da sheep. Den she saw dat skinwalker running away and found me. Ever since den I've been really scared."

"You don't have to be afraid anymore," promised Kee. "Just stay by me!"

Annie, for that was her name, did stay by him. After the squaw dance was over, they moved into an old hogan, belonging to Kee's great-grandma, which had been abandoned for years. Even though she had not died in it, which would have rendered it a taboo to use, it was close to the place Aunt Betty had been struck by lightning, and the rest of the family had no interest in it.

Great-grandma's house was in need of much personal attention, and the new couple busied themselves with the work of chinking the gaps between the logs, clearing out mice nests, and picking up the garbage left by drunks who had spent a night en route to another wild party.

Kee and Annie were pleased with each other. Both were industrious and attractive, but there was much that they did not know, unknown things that would later haunt them.

Annie had lived in a rough home situation. Her dad had sold her mother's favors to other men for money and alcohol. Witnessing this had created a wounded rage within her that she directed against her dad, his twisted friends, and any other man who reminded her of them. She had suffered through the experience with her younger sister and brother until she was old enough to move to Winslow and live with her aunt. It was there that she had gotten a job and learned how to be a social drinker.

She had seen plenty of alcohol abuse in her childhood, and at first was very cautious about using it. Lately, though, she had developed a strong taste for the stuff, though she felt no need of it now that she was happily with a good man.

Kee, on the other hand, was still sober and very wary of using any kind of brew. He did not want to tell her of his past for fear that it would spoil their relationship. He also did not know how to express his feelings—to her or anyone else. Moreover, he wanted to provide for Annie, and his railroad money was not going to last very long.

Without even a horse, Kee thought about hitching a ride to Moab and finding a used car. He had learned the basics of driving while working on the railroad when all his friends got drunk. In the beginning he was almost as dangerous as his inebriated buddies. Their hoots and hollers were sometimes helpful as he tried to navigate his way across the little towns. But after several occasions as the designated driver, he developed a basic ability to control the car.

Now he needed wheels. Outside of sheepherding for food, employment was nearly nonexistent. His mind carefully weighed the options. They could move to a border town along the edge of the reservation and try to find work, but it was hard for uneducated Navajos to get jobs that paid enough to live on. Plus, he had heard bad things about how some of the border townspeople treated his people. If he had a vehicle he could drive to work in a border town and come home after work to Annie and the hogan. One evening he shared his thoughts with her, and she liked the plan. They had no furniture, cooking utensils, or food, so she wanted to go with him.

The next rising sun found them in the back of a pickup, hitching a ride toward Moab. As the driver kindly dropped them off in front of a well-known car dealer, Kee gave him $2 then turned to look at the cars. In two short hours Kee and Annie were driving off the car lot in a faded Chevy Impala. It had taken all but $50 of Kee's savings, and with the remaining money he filled the gas tank, took Annie to lunch, and bought some groceries.

Everything was going fine until Kee started looking for work. Eight rejections later (even from places that had "Help Wanted" signs), the sun was moving closer to the western horizon. The couple left Moab and tried several other towns along the way. Monticello and Blanding gave him the same response. He had heard about prejudice before, but this was the clearest sense of it that he'd ever known. Even places needing a dishwasher had turned him down.

They rode back to the reservation with mixed emotions. Annie was pleased to have groceries and their car. Her parents had never owned a motorized vehicle, so the novelty of it was exciting. A growing bitterness welled up within Kee, coming out of the pain of his rejections in the workplace. He felt what every caring, unemployed family man has felt—fear. It was a fear that comes from the thought of letting those down who depend on you. In his mind he imagined Annie being hungry, and quickly turned to a more positive channel. Perhaps in Page, Arizona, he would find work.

Before they returned to the old hogan, they stopped by Annie's family place in Moon Water. There she gathered her few personal items, the weaving materials, and loom. She was serious about this relationship with Kee and was going to do all she could to help out.

After they had loaded everything into the Impala, Kee decided to drive over to his cousin Jim's place a half mile down the road. Jim, the Vietnam vet that Kee had greatly envied, had returned from his tour of duty shortly after Kee had gone off to work for the railroad.

The car pulled up to a lone mobile home next to an outhouse. Three dogs ran out, barking their greetings. Kee honked the horn and waited in the car for a response from the house. In the old days, a Navajo horseman would ride several times around a hogan, and if no one came out, he would ride off, assuming that it was not a good time to visit.

The door opened, and Jim peered out. He was not familiar with Kee's car and was trying to determine who was in it. Kee could sense that he was drunk and wasn't sure he wanted to visit anymore. But he figured he would spare Annie by leaving her in the car while he had just a short visit with his cousin. He got out without a word. She sensed Jim's condition, too, and had no desire to go in for a visit.

After the usual greeting, Jim opened the door and invited Kee inside. Kee hesitated for a moment, but decided to enter Jim's trailer. His wife and children seemed frightened and depressed, and Jim was loud and overly-friendly.

"Hey, bro! Sit down right here—my bess chair! Juss for you!"

Kee took his seat after shaking the hands of each family member. He didn't know what to say, so he kept quiet for a few moments. Jim started in again.

"Hey, bro! Nice wheels you got. You could make some money! Dat trunk can hold a lotta beer! Man, I pay a stinkin' $2 for a good-size bottle . . . I shoulda use my GI money to buy me a car insteada dis trailer. I got a wife and kids who don' even respeck me!" Jim glared at his family huddled in the corner of the living room. His wife started crying.

"Now see? Dar she goes again!" Jim's mood was changing quickly. "Don' cry for what I say! It's true! Tell him—tell him how you hate me! Tell him how I messed up your life! Go ahead!"

Jim got up and staggered over to his weeping wife. A sickening feeling came over Kee. He had seen this scenario before somewhere in his childhood. He knew that abuse would happen if he didn't do something.

"Jim!" he called. And then more softly: "Come on out and show me how I could fit that beer in my car."

Jim needed little encouragement for such a venture. He turned and wobbled toward Kee and the door. As he reached for the door knob, Kee shot a meaningful glance at Jim's wife and motioned with his chin toward the door on the opposite side. She seemed to understand, and Kee left with a small sense of relief.

Out at the car Jim seemed more interested in Annie than in where to put the beer. But Kee made it clear that Annie was his lady. As the two stood outside, Jim made an offensive remark about her, and Kee figured he had bought Jim's wife and children enough time to escape out the other door.

"Thanks for your help, my cousin-brother. I'll see you later."

With that, Kee jumped quickly into the car, started the engine, and slammed it into gear. Jim stood stupefied for a moment then lunged at the car as it sped off. Just missing the rear bumper, he hit the ground hard and lay for a while in the red dust.

Annie said little on the way back to the old hogan, and Kee did the same. It had been a long day, and each one debriefed themselves in their own private reflections. It was a barrier that seemed so hard to cross.

They were up early the next day. Kee was going to Page to look for work, and Annie was setting up her loom. When she told him to come home early and eat with her, he gave her a promising smile.

Page was no better than Moab for Kee. He went from business to business before getting discouraged around 2:00 in the afternoon. Frustration and desperation were taking over. He knew that he couldn't continue to put gas in the car without money coming in, and Jim's suggestion kept coming into his mind. He never wanted to be like Jim, but he might be able to use Jim's idea to make the money that he needed to take care of Annie. His mind flitted back to Aunt Mary's long-gone boyfriend and his shiny pickup. Perhaps if he became a bootlegger he'd even be able to buy himself a nice pickup!

The next morning he donned his silver concho belt and bracelets, a gift he had gotten for himself after his summer working in the potato fields. He headed for the pawn shop and exchanged them for cash. It was the Navajo credit card. He now had enough to fill the gas tank—and buy a trunk full of beer.

He was uneasy as he drove back to the old hogan. He didn't know what to expect from Annie when she saw the beer. He didn't even want to tell her about it. Perhaps he wouldn't have to.

Annie was happy to see him, but she quickly sensed that something was wrong. The warmth of his usual greeting had diminished slightly. She assumed that it was connected to problems in Page.

"No jobs in Page?" she queried.

"Nothing."

"It's OK; we have a home and food. Come; eat!"

Inside, the smell of roasted meat greeted him, and she handed him a large piece. As he munched, he noticed that the loom was assembled across from where they slept. She followed his eyes and proudly showed the section of the rug that she had managed to weave during the day. Kee gave a soft compliment about its beauty, and Annie was even more pleased. She had put much of her own soul into its complex design. When Kee was nearly finished eating, she spoke again.

"I found some yucca growing and got some roots. Den I borrowed a pan and a bowl from your mom. We can wash our hair now."

It was the old but good way for a couple to get clean. When mixed with water, the pieces of yucca make a strong soap that can irritate the eyes. Annie helped Kee wash and rinse his hair. Using the basin and bowl, she poured bowl after bowl over his bent head until his hair was thoroughly clean. It was the only way to get running water in the hogan. After Kee finished bathing, he returned the favor. As he did so he felt fortunate to have such a beautiful and caring woman. She was a medicine to his wounded soul. His mood had changed. The beer in the trunk was temporarily forgotten.

Late the next morning the couple stirred themselves after the sun was high in the sky. Kee dressed hurriedly, grabbed a few pieces of roasted meat, and headed for the door.

"Where are you going?" Annie asked.

"To get some money. Goodbye!" he said as he rushed outside.

She stared after him, wondering at his brisk farewell after such tender moments the night before. She wondered if it had meant as much to him as it had to her.

The car fired up easily, but Kee's mind was not at peace. He knew he had to get rid of the beer and make it pay. But where to start? He knew he couldn't sell to relatives. They would want him to give it to them for free. Nor could he try to sell around the tribal police. They would put him in jail for a day and take his booze away.

He drove to some neighbors whom he knew liked to drink. When the occupants of the hogan came out, he had no trouble selling some of his wares. The next house didn't quite have enough cash to cover what they wanted, so they traded him some cooking pots and dishes. Soon his confidence was up, and he began selling to strangers in hogans he'd never visited before. His beer was going fast, and both his pockets and the back seat of the car were filling up. By the time he was almost out of beer, he had a blanket, the dishes and pots, a lantern, a live chicken in a cardboard box, an old sturdy ax, and $83 in cash.

By early afternoon he was hungry as he headed back to the old hogan. His mood was playful as he unloaded the items and brought them inside. Annie was sitting at the loom. She had made more progress, but her interest shifted to what Kee was bringing in.

"Where did dis come from?"

"These are wedding gifts!"

"From whom?"

"Come on; I'll drive you to the trading post," Kee said in an attempt to change the subject.

It only partially worked. Annie was ready for a break, and a trip to the trading post was always a good thing. She rose and inspected the items as she readied herself. They drove off, leaving the chicken in the box on the shady side of the hogan.

Kee was pleased with what he was able to purchase for Annie at the trading post. It made him feel good to get her the things she wanted, yet he was careful to save enough for a tank of gas and another trunk load of beer. He knew he had to tell her soon, but the thought only made him feel sick. So he pushed it out of his mind.

There was plenty to carry as they headed back to their car. He opened the trunk to put the sacks of groceries in—and there sat the one remaining six-pack of beer.

"Is dat a wedding gift too?" Annie asked with a cool stare.

Kee struggled in silence. Part of him wanted to tell another lie, but another part of him was grieved and wanted to come clean with her.

"It's better to talk in the car," he said.

As Kee told her the whole story, Annie listened in silence. He assured her that he didn't want to drink any, he just wanted to sell it until they could get good jobs. Her response surprised him.

"So dis six-pack is for me den."

Kee was relieved but a little uncomfortable. He didn't like the thought of her drinking. They had been in harmony with everything they had done so far. The thought of not being in unity bothered him, yet he also wanted to please her.

"I was just thinking of selling it to others . . . But if you really want one, go ahead."

As they unloaded, Kee noticed her taking one of the beers and downing it quickly. It bothered him. Part of him wanted to join her, but another part was sickened and afraid.

Night was approaching. After putting the groceries away, they brought the chicken and its box inside and bolted the old door shut. As they began to feast on their provisions, a loud knock interrupted them. Kee and Annie looked at each other. Kee arose and opened the door to a drunk neighbor, swaying in front of him.

"Hello! I need shum more beer, and I got money!"

Kee thought about the beer in his trunk and decided it was a good time to get rid of it. He walked out to the car, opened the trunk, and sold the man the last five bottles. The man staggered off, and Kee returned to his meal. He wasn't sure if he liked this anymore.

They finished their feast and went to bed, but their rest was short-lived. Another loud knock came at midnight, making both of them jump. Another neighbor wanted to buy more beer. Though Kee called out, telling the man that he had no more, the man continued pounding on the door and asking for beer. Kee didn't want to go outside and get into a fight while driving the man off, so he waited for the drunk to give up. It took so long that he was about ready to go outside when the man finally left.

Kee and Annie sank back into an uneasy sleep. Triggered by the unwelcome visitors, unpleasant dreams stirred up from the unprocessed memories in their childhood experiences troubled them.

CHAPTER 10

The Way to the Bottom

"There is a way that seems right to a man, but in the end it leads to death"
(Proverbs 14:12, NIV).

IN THE GRAY LIGHT OF DAWN Kee and Annie awoke feeling ill. The stress of the night before and the poor sleep left them with the unhappiness they had always known before coming together. Even though they could now feel love, it hadn't changed their world. The same harsh reality, the same fearful loneliness, existed in the silence as they dressed and prepared for the day.

A stolen glance at Annie's beautiful form had left Kee with an inner rush of wonder. She was so lovely, and yet he sensed her emotional fragility. He wanted to open all the feelings of his heart, to tell her his whole life story with every dark detail, but he was afraid. The thought of losing her because of something that he said, made the risk too great to take.

So with painful restraint, he silently resolved not to be transparent with her. Perhaps sometimes he would, out of necessity affirm his love for her, but not too often—his affection might be viewed as weakness. Besides, it was not the way that he had been raised. Affection throughout his childhood had been given more in a look, or the tone of voice when his nickname (Ashkee) had been spoken. Phrases such as "I love you" were rarely used. So the longing of his inner soul for expression continued to haunt him.

Kee's grandma had always used corn pollen in her morning prayers. She climbed a small hill, carrying a bit of the pollen she had collected from the garden. Kee had often gone with her when he was little and listened to her good words. It hadn't meant much more to him than just another pleasant memory. But now, for some reason, it formed a picture in his mind. In the coolness of the new day he knew he needed something. But they had no pollen. How could he pray without pollen? The Anglo people didn't use pollen to pray, he remembered. They didn't seem to need it. But he didn't know how to pray their way.

He pushed the whole subject out of his mind. He had many miles to cover, and he wanted to prepare Annie. "I'm going to Cortez," he began. "Keep the ax with you. If anybody else comes for trouble, you know how to use it."

"When are you coming back?" She didn't want him to go, but felt it would be weakness to admit her fear.

"Before sundown." Kee fired up the Impala and headed for Colorado. He would be in between the four sacred mountains all day. It should be OK—even for a bootlegger. The way it worked in the four corners area was to use different routes to purchase alcohol and, thereby, avoid the suspicions of the tribal police who watched for vehicles making regular runs to town.

Once in Cortez, it didn't take him long to buy more fuel and booze. The prices were good, and he made mental notes on where he might return to go shopping with Annie. The whole circuit of returning and selling took less time than he had imagined. People recognized the car now, and many came over quickly to purchase the beverage. This time he received more cash, and he made sure his trunk was empty of beer before he returned to the old hogan.

Annie was relieved to see him back early. No one had bothered her during the day, and she was happy when he wanted to take her to the trading post again. On the previous trip there had been several things she had wanted to buy, but Kee had said, "Next time." Her misgivings from the previous night were strong, but the trip to the trading post pushed those nagging doubts into a dark corner of her mind.

Before the sun had lowered itself to the edge of the sky, Kee and Annie were back at the hogan and busy unloading all kinds of treasures. They were two children in young adult bodies, delighted that many things they had always wanted were now theirs.

That night only one visitor came to the hogan. He was reasonable, and left in a short while. They told themselves that this was not a problem. They slept better, though Kee did have another disturbing dream that he could not remember in the morning.

Thus, the cycle began and continued. For weeks it was only accented by a greater number of visitors on some nights. Kee finally purchased a shotgun to chase the violent ones off. The Impala now had several dents and a crack in the windshield as evidence of several stressful incidents.

Annie didn't ask for more alcohol, and Kee was relieved. Their happiness continued to grow when she became pregnant. The thought of a child was most delightful to Annie, who spent so much time alone at the hogan, and Kee fancied the thought of being a dad. He wanted to give what he had never received. But a wind was beginning to erode the beautiful sand painting of their lives, starting at the edges as a warning.

The temperatures dropped below freezing just before a snowstorm hit. Kee had made a beer run that day and was feeling smug about his situation. He had beat the snow, and they had plenty of firewood.

The next morning crunching footsteps and a knock at the door brought immediate apprehension to both of them. When the caller rapped a second time, he opened the door a crack. Wind and snow rushed in, and the morning light shone upon the face of his mother.

"Hello, my mother; come in!"

Mother was visibly upset. It was obvious that she had been crying.

"Your auntie Mary is dead." They found her dis morning down by da highway. She was frozen. She kicked dat bootlegger out, and den she started walking around more. She was always trying to find alcohol." Mother gave Kee a knowing look.

They had never discussed his business, but he guessed that she knew. Now she seemed to be blaming him. He felt defensive. He had avoided his aunt since his return from Phoenix, and he had never sold or given any beer to her. He didn't want to have her bumming off him. But what if he *had* given her free beer? Maybe she wouldn't have died out by the highway.

A wave of guilt and shame washed over Kee. He fought to avoid the sinking feeling. It wasn't his fault! He hadn't made her drink! He had done nothing against his aunt. "I am sad" was his only response.

Mother didn't stay long. She had others to tell and arrangements to make. She had heard that the people at the Monument Valley Seventh-day

Adventist Church had helped people in the community dig graves and give funeral services, and she had to find them. She, like most of her people, was afraid of having much to do with handling the dead.

After Mother left, Kee continued to wrestle with his thoughts and feelings. Annie sensed that he was agitated and, in her inadequacy, avoided saying anything to him. In her fear, she kept a distance that only served to lock his suffering inside.

▼ ▼ ▼

The funeral service was a crowded occasion. Relatives, friends, and old drinking buddies all came to pay their last respects to Aunt Mary. A Navajo funeral was more than a meeting at the church. It included the family taking shovels and burying their loved one in some lonely spot. The men of the family piled and smoothed a mound of dirt equal to the amount of soil displaced by the wooden coffin above the gravesite of the deceased. Then the women relatives decorated the mound with water, food, and pretty things. Afterward, everyone went somewhere to eat.

In the blur of day-long events one thing stood out in Kee's mind. The preacher at the Seventh-day Adventist church had said some unusual things about the dead. He used a chapter from the Bible in which the Great One, Jesus Christ, had said that the dead man, Lazarus, was sleeping. He continued the story and showed that not only was Christ powerful over death but He would also wake up the dead at the end of the world.

It was a hopeful thought for Kee. He thought of his aunts, Mary and Betty. The chapel people at the Indian school were always saying that those who didn't become Christians were going to hell right away and burning forever. It had seemed unfair that God would do that to his dear aunt Betty. The traditional Navajo religion didn't offer any hope, either. The thought of being reunited at the end of the world was a comfort to his sad heart.

The sequence of trouble only intensifies when the wrong spirit is leading. A few days later Kee came home to find Annie with a troubled face. He looked at her carefully and wondered if he'd done something that she was upset about. But it was not about him.

"Your mother came over again," she began. "She brought bad news about your cousin Jim." She paused, and Kee braced himself for the worst. "He got upset when he was drunk, and he shot himself—in front of his kids."

Kee was stunned beyond expression. He knew by her look that she had spoken the truth, but the sickening feeling that engulfed him was too great to bear. It made an imprint that marked him beyond all future good times. No matter where he would go, he would carry the pain of that terrible moment when he pictured the news of his cousin, his nieces, and nephew.

He bowed his head then shook it in an attempt to clear the violent vision from his mind. It did clear enough to picture the day before, when he had given his cousin some beer. He had sold so much already that he thought he'd stop by to visit and share his success. Of course, he didn't know if it was his beer that had caused his cousin's death, but the guilt of his involvement hung about him like a chain. He had hated many things before, but now he truly hated himself.

On their last visit together Jim had talked to Kee about his guilt over what he had done in Vietnam. The warfare had been so vicious that after one of his dear buddies had been killed, he started shooting even helpless women and children. He shared his anger about being called "chief" by the other soldiers, and spoke with pride about how they all depended on him to lead them in the dangerous combat missions. He had always been able to spot the ambushes and traps. Then his conversation came back to what he had done and how terrible he felt about it. Kee wanted to help his cousin but didn't know how. So he just passed him another beer.

Sitting in the Adventist church for another funeral, he heard the preacher talk about the love of the Creator-God, how that love could heal anything and save anyone. Kee wondered about this. The chapel people had said that suicide was a sure way to go to hell. But the idea of God's love reaching down to save any man was a more beautiful way. It gave him hope for his cousin and for himself. He didn't know how to obtain it, but the encouraging words kindled in his mind the thought that maybe Someone really did care. Though it didn't change anything for Kee, the seeds of hope often lie dormant for many a season.

Weeks passed, and Kee continued to peddle his booze. As Annie's delivery time drew near, she became more aware of the little person growing within her. She focused on her preparations for that little one and unconsciously withdrew from her man. Kee sensed it too. A cradleboard was purchased, and she made many trips over to her mother's place. More often than not, she was absent from the old hogan by the time Kee returned from his beer runs.

When a woman gave birth to a baby their people always said "she had a baby for him," in reference to the child's father. Kee knew this, but it seemed of little value if she was no longer available. Self-pity brewed within him. There was already too much loss stored up in his heart not to take this personally. He no longer felt important to her. Now he was merely a source of income.

When the evening arrived for her to go to the hospital, Kee drove her to the same hospital where he had been born. There was no place for dads in the birthing process in those days, and Kee felt a need to watch over their place anyway and returned to the hogan. They still were visited by unruly visitors in the night hours.

That night visitors did come, the kind that are hard for a man to deal with. A nice car drove up to the old hogan and honked demandingly. Kee came outside and found a car full of women who were drinking. They had been driving by when they noticed his Impala, and since they had gotten beer from him before, they thought they'd stop by and share with him.

"Hey!" cried several voices in various stages of drunkenness. "We have beer for *you* this time!"

"I don't need it. Go home!" Kee replied firmly.

"Aw," one attractive young tribal employee whined, "he's not very friendly. Come on; let's go!"

"No!" protested others. "Let's give him a drink; he needs some cheer to help him, some good medicine for grouchy guys!"

"Here," said the first woman, handing him an opened beer can.

"No thanks. You better go home."

"Aw, see? He's just like that. Come on; let's go find someone friendlier."

The car sped off in a cloud of dust, and Kee almost wished they had stayed as he walked back inside the lonely hogan. They were all young, educated, and attractive girls. He tried to think about Annie, but this proved difficult. They'd had an unresolved squabble over the business. Kee wanted to quit bootlegging and move to a big city where he could do something else. Annie, now that she was about to deliver, wanted to be close to her mother's family and also had become dependent on their lifestyle. Kee resented the way she treated him whenever they disagreed on an issue.

He thought again about the carload of girls. He had never been approached like that before. It felt good to know that they were interested in him. Before long he again heard the sound of a car, and obnoxious honking came again. With no plan but to be more friendly he strode outside once more and faced the carload of females.

"Hey, tall man," called one of the passengers, "why don't you like to have fun?"

Kee didn't like the loud voices, so he walked over to the driver's window, thinking it might help them not feel the need to be so noisy. The smells of perfume and beer hit him in a powerful combination.

"You girls are too drunk," he calmly began. "Why don't *you* stop driving around so you don't get into a wreck?"

"No, no," one of them retorted. "Why don't you drive us around so we don't get in a wreck?"

Kee paused. He hadn't thought of such an option. He didn't have anyone to stay home with. Perhaps it would be good to drive for these girls and keep them from getting into an accident. He was aware of their attractiveness but told himself it would be OK—just to help them.

"OK," he agreed. "I will drive for you."

Shouts and hoots greeted his response. The driver pushed the girl next to her over and made way for Kee. He opened the door and climbed in, even as Annie was being helped onto the delivery table some miles away.

The rest of the night was a gradual surrender of first one kind and then another for Kee. At first he had tried to take the girls to their homes, but they made a game of giving the wrong directions to him. They finally got him laughing with them and accepting their beer. Their shady jokes and physical advances became easier to accept. Then as the alcohol took over, it all became a hilarious fog fading into nothingness.

Kee awoke, trying to figure out where he was, as the full impact of a giant headache hammered in his brain. When he lifted his head and stared, things came into better focus. There were blanketed forms all around him, sleeping in this strange hogan. Then he remembered the night before and got out from under the blanket he'd obviously been sharing. He noticed that many articles of his clothing were piled up nearby, and he quickly put them on before anyone else could awaken. His fear and shame were real, but no one even stirred. As he stepped over the sleepers, he remembered Annie at the hospital. The claws of guilt took an iron grip on his heart. Opening the door, he stepped into the winter's noonday sun. The chilly wind bit into his cotton shirt. He heard a moan behind him as he closed the door.

The car he had driven the night before was parked right in front of him. Looking around at the lay of the land, he got his bearings and began jogging down the red clay road. The snow, now replaced by mud, had melted so that it could only be seen under the bushes. Kee slipped and slid as he jogged along. His headache was tremendous, but he pressed on, punishing himself.

When he finally reached the Impala in front of the old hogan, he suddenly became worried. Had he lost his keys in the night? Checking his pants pockets, he felt a sudden relief as his hand touched the small metal objects. Soon he was rolling down the road toward Monument Valley Hospital. The towering red columns of sandstone pointed upward, reminding him of how low he was.

It was almost 2:00 in the afternoon when he parked the car. Quickly glancing in the rearview mirror, he smoothed his hair down with spit and climbed out. Walking up the steps, he felt a growing apprehension, a great fear of Annie finding out. He didn't want to lose her, and thought he would be able to excuse himself with a made-up story.

When he entered her room, he was greeted with a lovely sight. There was Annie, nursing his baby daughter in a sweet, tender moment he would never forget. Annie lifted her beautiful eyes to him in a searching sadness. Neither spoke for several moments.

Kee, bound by inner conflict, wanted to express his joy and gratitude to Annie about the baby, but he needed to apologize. He wanted to rush over and join them, but he felt unworthy and out of place.

"My Babe," he said, not remembering that there were now two who qualified for that title. "I'm sorry I'm late. Some people came over, and it took a long time for them to leave." He stepped closer and leaned over the bed to kiss Annie and look at the baby.

"Who came over?"

"Uncle Johnny from Navajo Mountain came last night with his oldest boy." Kee figured that would be a safe name to use since they had never been to that out-of-the-way place before.

"What's dat red mark on your neck? It looks like you got a bite."

Kee felt his facial temperature rise. He hadn't thought to look in the mirror at his neck. While he hesitated Annie continued.

"My older sister went by da old hogan dis morning and she said nobody was dare—just da car. She came by to tell you da good news." Annie broke into sobs, and the tiny baby stopped feeding and joined in.

It was more than Kee could bear. He tried to talk to her and apologize, but she was too shaken to listen. A nurse came in and suggested that he not disturb the mother further and that he leave. Kee agreed but promised that he would be back.

Now he felt even worse. Suicide would have been too good for him now. In his shame and remorse, he wanted to try to make up for what he had done and support Annie, even if he was never able to win her back.

He got in the car and headed off to buy more beer. At least he knew Annie liked his money. But now there was a greater sense of guilt and shame. With nowhere else to go, he began medicating himself with the alcohol. It seemed to give him a sense of comfort when there was nothing else around. But he promised himself that he would never allow himself to get drunk; he would control it.

During Annie's hospital stay Kee worked hard at bootlegging. He had several close encounters with the tribal police but had always managed to elude them on the dirt trails that led through the treacherous washes. Business was good, and he had a good stack of money by the time she was discharged. He had made daily visits with her favorite treats and gifts made by the silversmith. Gradually, she had seemed friendlier, and by the time of her discharge she was ready to go home with Kee. Her options were limited anyway—every bed in the crowded homes of her relatives was in use.

Happily Kee took her and baby Carlita home. He opened the door and proudly showed them the new double bed and playpen that he'd purchased. Annie was pleased, and little Carlita, in her cradleboard, made no complaints.

Life moved on. The only difference now was Baby Carlita and the nightly six-pack that the couple would consume together. Sometimes it was a pleasant thing, but there were also frequent arguments and accusations that came out when they were drinking. Apparently these episodes were louder than they realized, because one morning there was a knock on the door. When Kee opened it, he looked down on his small, sturdy mother.

"You gotta go, my son. Eber since dat girl came here, we hab a lotta bad people comin' ober here. And now we can hear her yellin' at you. It's not good for da baby, and it's not good for you, my son. I am sad, but you have to move someplace else."

Kee stood silently and listened. He had never heard her speak more tenderly to him, and yet she was evicting him. He nodded. Sadness was in his heart as he watched her walk away. Turning to look inside, he saw Annie's expression and knew she had heard too. There was an angry resoluteness in her face as she began to pack things up. Kee felt fear when she was angry and decided not to say anything.

He went outside to gather some things together. He figured they could tie everything—even the mattresses—onto the outside of the car and make it in one load. His mind raced through their options. The tribal police were on to him in this area. Maybe a new start on the southeast side of the reservation would be good for them.

When the car was loaded, Kee discussed his idea with Annie, and she agreed. She was tired of the area, and there was no room for them at her family's place. They drove away from the old hogan, not knowing they were leaving forever. They headed toward their people's capital, Window Rock. The up-thrust of the Chuska Mountains had been a natural fortress during centuries of invasions against the Diné. Its tree covered shoulders were always beautiful to look upon, and the young couple was comforted as they passed by them.

Kee stopped in Window Rock and bought a Gallup newspaper. It advertised a number of places for rent, and after making some phone calls and driving around, they chose a small, dilapidated house between Window Rock and Gallup. It was on a dirt road just off the highway, among the juniper trees and sagebrush.

With Gallup so close, Kee could sometimes fill up his trunk with beer twice in one day. Sales were always good, and Annie enjoyed the shopping trips to town. Carlita had outgrown her cradleboard, and one of

Annie's sisters had moved into the spare bedroom. Alcohol use continued in the home with the same results. Yet it seemed to be the only way that they could ever manage to laugh or be intimate anymore.

Kee kept himself numb most of the time. It had become his main consolation. This White man's medicine was good at that. But it also slowed his driving reaction time until it finally caught up with him. On an eastbound curve coming out of Window Rock one day he overcorrected and left the road. It wasn't the first time he had gone out into the bushes, but this time he went over a steep embankment and rolled the car. As it became airborne, Kee let go of the steering wheel and put his hands around his head to protect himself from objects flying about inside the car.

Then suddenly it was over. The roof had been mashed down, but he managed to crawl out through the broken rear window. The car was demolished. His survival was a miracle, but he didn't know it. The car contained no evidence of bootlegging, as he had been on his way to purchase more beer. But Kee knew that he was drunk enough to go to jail, so he began walking down the road.

He had walked for a long time before he realized that he didn't have one of his shoes on. He assumed it had been lost during the accident. Shortly after this discovery a pickup pulled over for him, and he gratefully climbed into the back, which was full of good-time Charlies going to Gallup for more fun. Kee laughed and joked with them all the way to Gallup, where they immediately went to a bar.

They soon discovered that the men already inside the bar had no love for Indians. As Kee and his friends entered, comments were made, and the mood changed quickly. Within minutes a huge brawl ensued, the fight racially divided among the Anglos, Mexicans, and Native Americans of various tribes. Kee found himself involved in a battle that he hadn't foreseen, but he quickly grabbed a chair, sweeping it about with powerful strokes to clear away his opponents. The battle continued even after the police arrived. Ironically, the ones who started the carnage were not apprehended. Kee and most of his friends were taken to the jail in handcuffs.

It was a long night, not as fun as he remembered when his buddies had joined him in Oklahoma. The next day he was arraigned in court and given the choice of a $100 fine or 100 days in jail. In his earlier stupor Kee had forgotten his stash of cash in the demolished Impala. Now he had no way to pay his way out of jail. Glumly he returned to his cell and sat with his head in his hands. A hundred days was a terribly long time. He wouldn't be free until after Christmas. He wondered what would happen to Annie and Carlita. They didn't even know where he was.

Christmas . . . His thoughts wandered to religious things. Maybe he should quit this alcohol medicine all together and find a better kind. He didn't know any chants for getting out of jail. He remembered that the chapel people had always stressed that Jesus was just a prayer away, and that He could hear anyone. Grandpa had told him that the White man's religion was not the Navajo way. Well, jails were not the Navajo way either. Maybe he needed the White man's God to help him out of this one.

With his head still in his hands, he softly spoke his first prayer to Jesus. Other inmates noticed, but none of them cared enough to bother him. When he had finished, he felt better and lay down to sleep.

The next morning an officer opened the cell door and called his name. Kee followed apprehensively as he was led to a desk. A clerk was talking to a very tall White man. The clerk pointed at Kee and asked if this was the one. The tall man nodded and began pulling $20 bills out of his wallet.

Within minutes Kee was walking outside with the man. When they entered the parking area, the tall man turned to him. "You can walk a better road from here." With that he turned and walked away. Kee put his head down. He felt as if the man knew everything about him, and it caused him shame. Moments later he lifted his head to watch the man walking off, but he was gone. The street was empty, and there was nowhere he could have gone in that short space of time. Amazed, Kee took a few steps in the direction the man had taken and then stopped. It was not the direction he needed to go to catch a ride back home.

He headed for the place he knew he could easily hitch a ride. Still in a state of wonder, he climbed into the back of the pickup that pulled over for him. It had been a supernatural event for him, he knew. The only supernatural events that he had known about before were negative and frightening ones.

Kee's demolished car had been towed away to a junkyard, and it took several days to locate it. When he arrived at the lot, they did allow him to retrieve his personal items. Some were missing, but gratefully no one had found his stash of cash. Once back home, Kee had some explaining to do.

With a missing car and bruised face from the fight, he could only tell the truth. Finishing with the tall man story, he pressed the point that he had made a decision to go a different direction. Their neighbor, a medicine man, had sensed a power that attended Kee. More than once he had offered Kee an apprenticeship with him. Now Kee told Annie that he was ready to go that way. The story of the tall man had impressed Annie deeply also. She inwardly hated their destructive cycle. So in the momentum of the moment, she joined him in the commitment to change.

The medicine man was pleased. He had a large following and saw Kee's power as a valuable asset. Kee joined him as he was called to help people with problems. Some were sick, some needed to have their house blessed, and others needed help to fight the witchcraft that was being used against them by others. Kee helped in many ceremonies. He made it a point to do whatever the medicine man said. Learning the songs was a major challenge. Ceremonies held in dirt-floored hogans frequently lasted all night. But a greater challenge was the lack of money. The medicine man charged a fee for his services, a small percentage of which went to Kee. It was hard for the little family to live on the amount he was receiving. Compared to bootlegging it was poverty, and Annie had to sign up for food stamps.

Getting around now was harder, too. Hitchhiking to Gallup wasn't so bad, because the traffic was often sympathetic Navajos who had once been hitchhikers themselves. Often the weather was nasty, either in the hot or cold ends of the spectrum, so that the 15 to 30 minutes out by the roadside waiting for a ride was tough on Annie and Carlita.

In spite of the hardships, Kee enjoyed the uniqueness of being with a medicine man. He caught himself thinking that this was probably how it might have been for him as a child if his dad hadn't disappeared. But Kee was not a child now. He could never make up for what he had missed, and he could now see through the glamour of the medicine man's mystique. His time with the older man began to pay off in strange ways. He saw the arrogance and harshness and greed that lurked below the man's surface. This hurt Kee the most because it hurt his family.

Then one warm afternoon he came by the medicine man's house to ask for some badly needed money. The older man was sitting outside with a cold beer. The sight bothered Kee, but he approached anyway and explained his need for $20. He pointed out that he had not received anything for his assistance in the previous ceremony then waited for a reply. The older man claimed that he had no more money but offered him some beer to hold him over until the next ceremony.

Angrily, Kee told the man that he was through with the medicine man way and stomped off. "Da spirits hab called you!" the medicine man called out, a threatening note in his voice. "You can't run from dem!"

Kee didn't care what the old man said. He would find a better way. It had become clear to him that by staying with this man he would end up where he had been before. Returning to his home, he grabbed the concho belt and bracelets he had gotten out of the Page pawn shop, and hitched his way to Gallup.

These days Gallup always reminded him of the day he'd seen the tall man. He felt good going there, and after he had pawned his jewelry once more, he headed for the grocery store, knowing Annie and Carlita would be happy to see something besides bread and beans. As he walked along, he noticed a large tent that had been set up in an empty lot. He'd seen many revival tents out on the reservation—the Pentecostal churches pitched them every summer—and Kee had always avoided them because they turned the speakers up so loud they could be heard miles away. Some of the music was attractive, but the shouting preacher was the most offensive part of the program. This time, though, he remembered how the White man's God had helped him and decided he owed this God something.

He was warmly greeted by a friendly Anglo man who made casual conversation with him for a while, then the man mentioned that his translator was gone on a family emergency. He asked if Kee could help him translate the sermon into Navajo for the people. Kee had never tried such a thing before, but in the friendly environment he felt inclined to try.

As the meeting time approached, the music began to play. Kee enjoyed the happy songs, even if they were in English. He knew there were others who did not understand the words, and he felt sympathy for them. By the time the singing was finished, a good crowd had gathered.

As the speaker stood, he motioned for Kee to come stand beside him. Feelings of inadequacy and fear nearly overwhelmed him, but the man first prayed slowly, line by line, in English, and paused while Kee translated it into Navajo. The power of that prayer filled him as nothing else ever had.

A beautiful feeling of peace came over him, and for the next hour he stood beside the man and spoke beautiful words to the people.

When the speaker finished, he called for them to surrender to Jesus. Several people came forward, and the man prayed and dismissed the others. Then he and Kee visited with each person and prayed with them again. Finally everyone was gone, and Kee explained that he needed to be going also. Pastor Bob, as Kee would learn to call him later, placed his hands on Kee and prayed over him. He prayed about the past wounds, and for a new beginning with Jesus Christ. Kee felt tears fill his closed eyes, then overflow and make streaks down his cheeks. It felt so comforting and good to have this man praying for him. A picture of the medicine man charging for prayers came to his mind, but he squeezed his eyes more tightly shut, and refocused on the wonderful prayer the man was saying. When it was finished, Kee felt as though a 40-pound weight had been taken off his shoulders.

In simple words he expressed his gratitude to this wonderful man who, two hours earlier, had been a stranger. As he turned to leave, Preacher Bob stopped him and put a $20 bill in his hand. "The Lord told me to do this," he said simply.

Kee thanked the man again and left. A little fear tried to nag him about his late start home, but at the grocery store he was able to find a ride with another family that was heading back to the reservation.

Annie listened in wonder to Kee's account of the day. Her joy at the groceries and the extra money that Kee placed in her hand was natural. But the idea of joining a White man's religion was totally strange to her. Kee had invited her to join him on the following evening at the meeting, but she was noncommittal. Inwardly, though, she admitted that she liked Kee's enthusiasm and the positive results of the encounter. She had never seen him like this and liked the new man he seemed to be.

As for Kee, the world had changed. The lightness in his heart was something to treasure. It was higher than anything he had ever dreamed. It was deeper than the center of the earth. It was the most beautiful model of the universe that he'd ever known. He would learn more about this good medicine. But for now he would just savor it!

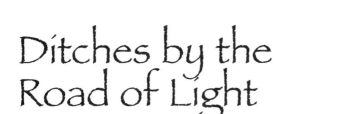

CHAPTER 11

Ditches by the Road of Light

"If we walk in the light, as he is in the light, we have fellowship with one another." (1 John 1:7, NIV).

K EE, COME HERE! Hurry! Der za snake under our bed!"

Annie's troubled voice was understood even before she had gotten all the words out. He rushed from the garden to the house and slowed as he passed her. She stood outside the low doorway, holding little Carlita in her arms.

"It's in da bedroom. Watch out!" she warned.

Kee snatched a broom just inside the doorway. Then he spied the cardboard box in which he'd brought home the groceries from Gallup the day before. The lights were on in the bedroom, so glancing about the floor to be sure the snake hadn't relocated itself, he bent over and used the broom handle to lift the low-hanging quilt. It was underneath the far side of the bed, up against the wall.

"I see you, Mr. Snake," Kee breathed softly, "and you have a lot of rattles!"

The large rattler stared from its coils, making no response other than to flick out its black tongue every few seconds. Kee tipped the grocery box sideways and scooted it over to his side of the bed, nearest the snake.

"Why did you go over to my side of the bed, Mr. Snake? Are you trying to scare me? It's not going to work!" Kee grasped the metal bed frame and quickly jerked the bed away from the wall.

An angry buzzing sound began. Kee made for the snake, leading with his broom. The rattler struck at it several times as it swept him into the box. Quickly, Kee tipped the box right side up and closed the flaps. Once the rattler found himself in the dark warm box, he began to feel safer and the buzzing soon stopped. Kee quietly put the broom away and came back for the box and its lethal contents. Bending his tall frame over, he gently lifted the box and made for the door. The snake made no further buzzing sound, as if with superior powers about, it thought it best not to inform anyone of its new location.

Annie watched wordlessly as Kee walked off into the cedar-covered hills. He walked a long way into the mountains. As he walked he realized that it was as if the evil curse of his entire life must be removed, and he walked farther. Finally, after an hour of walking, he gently placed the box on the ground, tipped it over, and opened the flaps.

The snake crawled out and wriggled into nearby bushes. Kee grabbed the box and returned home. Annie was still looking perplexed when he got home. He told her how far he had taken the snake and reassured her that it would be all right. But they both knew it was considered a bad omen by their people when a snake comes into a home. They normally would have gone quickly to get a medicine man to help them avoid the bad thing that was trying to happen, but now they were Christians. Wasn't that enough?

Kee went alone to Gallup that afternoon and attended the next meeting. The translator was still gone, and Kee was again asked to translate. Gladly he accepted, and for an hour let the wonderful words about Jesus and His plan to make our lives beautiful come out of his mouth. After he returned home, he gave a summary to Annie.

The next morning both of them went out into the garden to check on things. Kee noticed a movement in the pumpkin vines near Annie. "Stop!" he called. "Don't move!"

Annie froze. She didn't know what the problem was, but she could tell something was very wrong. Kee picked up a hoe and came to stand beside her. His eyes were riveted on a spot about four feet in front of her.

"Hold still!" he whispered. Then, as he began lifting the vines with his hoe, an aggravated buzzing sound began. This was followed by a pinging sound as the snake struck the hoe blade. Holding the vines high with his hoe, Kee knew the snake realized that it was vulnerable. As it tried to crawl away, Kee pinned it down as gently as he could with the hoe and told Annie to get the box.

Following the same procedure as the day before, he relocated this rattler. He walked back home, musing on the meaning of two rattlesnakes in two days. It was not a good sign. This snake seemed to have been meant for Annie. Was a former beer customer trying to curse them? Or was the old medicine man sending the snakes? Something was wrong and needed to be corrected. But how could he now do this? Would he be putting down his new faith if he went to a medicine man and had a ceremony done? Obviously, Kee would not go back to the same man who he'd once worked for. Should he find another one, or go to the preacher in Gallup?

He found Annie in the house and realized that she was more upset than the day before. Her beautiful eyes were framed with fear. "We got to do something. Somebody's trying to curse us!"

"I know," Kee replied, "but we don't have to be afraid of it. It only works if we believe it."

"We got to get some help!" Annie said, as tears welled up in her eyes.

"Yes, and we have to be strong and go to the preacher. We can ask him to come and pray for us and bless our place. If you come with me now we can talk to him and get him to come back here with us."

Annie still had her misgivings about the preacher, but the words Kee had shared with her on the previous night had touched her heart, and she was ready to try anything that might help their situation. She picked up Carlita and walked with Kee to catch a ride on the highway.

The tent was normally empty at this time of the day, but the preacher had felt impressed to have his morning's meditation under the canvas tent instead of in his office. Even more miraculous, he had spent far more time than the usual in prayer and was still there when Kee, Carlita, and Annie arrived.

At first he didn't hear them as he wordlessly prayed for the people. Then, hearing a soft rustling beside him, he looked up and arose from his knees, smiling. Gently he shook their hands, knowing that was the proper Navajo way, and turned expectantly toward Kee. There were many questions in the pastor's mind, but wisely he decided to wait. It would be too easy to make a verbal blunder with his sensitive guests.

Kee didn't introduce Annie and Carlita. He didn't remember much of the manners and social skills he had learned in the Indian schools. Besides, he was very concerned about getting help. His people believed that the more indirect you can be in making your point the better. So he launched into the history of the events leading up to this visit, even telling about his working for and finally leaving the medicine man, as well as the two snake incidents. He concluded with a simple summary of their need.

"We are needing help to get our house blessed and to find a way to stop this curse," he said simply.

The preacher had been around Kee's people long enough to know this manner of communication and had waited patiently to hear the entire story. Now it was his turn to speak.

"I am sorry to hear you are having trouble, but I know that Jesus can fix the problem for you. I would be happy to come over and pray to Jesus about this. When would be a good time for me to come?"

"Anytime," said Kee, hoping that it would be immediate.

"Well, then, how about now?"

"Sure!" said Kee, happiness rising in his heart.

The preacher quickly discovered that the Nez family had no transportation and offered to give them a ride in his own car.

Out at the little house the service was simple. The pastor explained that they must give the entire house, grounds, and their lives to a loving God. Then He would take care of them because they were His. He stressed that it was important to clean the house of anything that was from a different way—any way that was different from the simple love and power of Jesus Christ. Pastor Bob gave examples of things such as alcohol, drugs, bad books, music, and paraphernalia from other religions. In this way they would show respect for their heavenly Father and could be sure that it was only Jesus who had helped them.

Kee and Annie looked at each other. Then Kee got some medicine fetishes that the neighbor had given him and handed them to the preacher. Annie retrieved a charm that had been given to her, and some music tapes that she thought wouldn't fit with Jesus.

The pastor carried the items outside and laid them on the ground beyond the fence line. Then he came back to the house and said he would now do what God's ancient people in the Bible did to dedicate a holy place for Him. Taking out a bottle of olive oil, he prayed in each room, anointing the door posts, windows, and furniture with oil. Moving from room to room, praying aloud and using the name of Jesus Christ, he asked for beautiful things to happen in each room. Kee noted that he even put a little smudge of oil on the mirrors. Afterward he went outside with Kee, put a few drops of oil on the bottom of their shoes, and the two of them walked around the perimeter of the fence line, asking God to honor where they walked and protect the family within.

It was a complete service. Kee and Annie both felt much better as they rode back to Gallup with the pastor. At meeting time Kee continued his translation, and Annie sat in the back, drinking in the beautiful words of life. She was offered a Bible but declined, embarrassed by her poor reading skills. She thought it better to listen but say no to the Book from heaven than to accept it and be put on the spot and asked to find something in it or, worse, to be asked to read from it.

The days flew by. Pastor Bob and his wife, Marie, were easy to approach and always offered encouragement. Annie bonded immediately with Marie, and the two couples traveled around together, towing little Carlita along. Kee translated for Bob during their many visits to other homes and, in the process, he learned much. The pastor paid him for his time, and though it was not much, it was better than the medicine man had paid.

They began to grow closer, and their talk and laughter became more open and spontaneous. Soon a wedding was added to the discussions. It was more Pastor Bob and Marie's idea, but Kee and Annie went along with it in a state of wonderment. They had not pictured doing anything besides a medicine man's ceremony in a hogan; however, the money for such a ceremony was not easy to come by. Pastor Bob said he would help with the expenses, and so the dream was coming true—only it was now going to be a Christian wedding.

Both Kee and Annie had come to understand that Jesus, despite many artists' conceptions, was actually not a White man at all. He was a Brown man who spoke no English, and was from an ancient tribe of people who were more like their own people. The couple was more comfortable with this new Jesus they were learning about.

When the special day arrived, Kee donned his concho belt and turquois bolo tie. Pastor Bob had tried to get Kee and Annie to wear the traditional tuxedo and bridal gown, but only Annie had complied. The whole event was going to be strange enough for Kee without putting on clothing that would be artificial for him to wear. His identity was already set.

Kee and Annie met Pastor Bob and Marie at the church. After going to separate changing rooms, they shed their outer wear and put on white robes. Pastor Bob waited for them in the baptistery, where he stood in waist-deep warm water. He had explained to them how this was what Jesus had said people should do in order to make a new start. Kee and Annie both wanted this, and it seemed like the perfect way to begin a wedding day. The water's rushing sound and the warmth of being submerged felt good to Kee. He wanted to stay under longer! But time did not suspend its moments for the happy new man.

Walking down the aisle was not a big thing for Kee. Because of his translation work, he was now accustomed to being up front at church gatherings. But taking Annie's hand and looking for a few moments into her beautiful brown eyes was the climax of the event. He could hear the sound of Pastor Bob's voice and knew that he would need to say "I do" at the end, but his heart was being touched in a deeper way. The miracle of all that they'd been through to reach this spot—all the heartbreaks, fights, and loneliness—was now gone. Stirring within him was a gratitude that he thought would keep him faithful to her from that moment on. When it was his time to pledge himself he was ready, even though a large tear slid slowly down his cheek after he spoke the two small words.

After the wedding service, Kee and Annie received the bread and grape juice of the Holy Communion. Pastor Bob said this was one of the happiest days of his life; it was happier still for Kee and Annie. At the reception Kee spoke to the people:

"I feel like a new man! I am happy to make this new beginning with my wife. It's like a first day for us! It's a beautiful day. It's beautiful to be here. Thank you all for coming."

Annie smiled and tears gathered in her eyes. She never dreamed that they could make such a new, clean start together.

As the weeks rushed by, the four friends enjoyed many meaningful and happy events. Kee witnessed the love of God at work, and his faith strengthened. He was eager to learn and seemed to pick things up quickly. Pastor Bob was a simple man, sharing the basics with Kee.

Kee continued to dig deeper, seeking to see the parallels of the Gospel with his own Navajo way. That's how he one day remembered the ancient phrase "because He came, it is beautiful." Realizing that Jesus had made his life beautiful, he shared the insight with his dear Anglo friend.

"That's right, Kee!" Pastor Bob exclaimed. "Even if it originally was used for something else, it's really true about Jesus—He is out to make everything beautiful!"

Just as the beauty of one season always fades and another must be allowed to emerge, so it was with Kee's new religious experience. Several weeks later Pastor Bob dropped a bombshell.

"Kee, I have some hard news that I need to tell you." He paused, not knowing how best to say it. "I have been asked to take a church back east, and after praying about it, I accepted the call. Marie and I will be moving soon."

This was too much of a shock for Kee. He didn't understand that this was the way things go for pastors. The transient lifestyle for most Navajos was limited to the land between the Four Sacred Mountains. Even if a friend moved to the other side of the reservation and was not seen for a long time, it was comforting to know they were still only several hours away. The thought of this impending departure brought pain and misunderstanding.

"Did we do something to make you mad at us?" Kee asked.

"No, no, Kee! It's not like that. It's God leading us away to another place where He wants us to serve Him. We accomplished our mission here, and you and Annie are a big part of that!"

Kee said no more, but he thought about it incessantly and shared the news with Annie. She was more visibly upset than Kee had been. "It seems like everybody dat I love leaves me! Why does God want doze people back east to hear His word but not us Navajos?"

"Maybe the people back there are worse off than us," reasoned Kee, trying to give the benefit of the doubt to his friends. But in his heart the same question was nagging at him. Weren't all those areas already Christian? In Navajoland it wasn't that way.

After Pastor Bob and Marie left the congregation worked on the slow process of selecting a new pastor. Different members wanted different kinds of ministry, which led to division. Kee and Annie lost interest in the group when they saw them having such a struggle to work together. It didn't look like a loving family anymore. They thought of going to another church but were too discouraged to get themselves motivated.

Kee needed employment badly and managed to find a job with a Gallup furniture store, working as a bill collector on the reservation. The company had a vehicle that he was given to drive, and this made life easier for the family. Driving a nice pickup around on the reservation had advantages. Kee could get a load of coal at the mine and drop it off at the house, washing the truck before returning it to his employer. He could stop by the store and buy food so that Annie didn't have to walk or hitch a ride.

But the new life also had disadvantages. Kee and Annie were without the spiritual nurturing Pastor Bob and Marie had provided. Furthermore, they knew little about how to keep such an experience going on their own. Annie had depended on Marie for prayer support and found it harder to maintain her patience with Kee and Carlita. Kee did pray on his own, but his time with the Bible evaporated until he was not reading it at all. The resulting weakness was something he did not detect until it was too late.

One day as he drove out to an isolated hogan to collect money, he stewed over Annie's sharp words of that morning. It was not a new thing, though he didn't remember what had started it. It seemed that her new Christian life was slipping away. Of course, he didn't think about the condition of his own spirituality. His new wife had become like the old one. The distant feeling he had when around her was real, and he didn't know how to change it. He had tried to be intimate, but the rejection made it too painful to try again. A bitter edge gripped his heart as he spied the eight-sided structure in the distance where he was to make his collection. *Annie has given up everything we had,* he thought.

An attractive middle-aged woman met him at the door. Her loneliness and desperation made her less cautious with this tall, good-looking man. When Kee told her why he was there, she explained that she had no money. Kee used the technique he had been taught at the store and said, "You have to pay me something, or I will have to take all the new furniture back to the store."

The woman surprised him by inviting him in and offered him fresh mutton stew and fry bread. Kee accepted. He hadn't eaten a good meal in a long time. The woman served him, then sat nearby and told funny stories while Kee ate. Kee enjoyed the attention. He had been feeling like a lost puppy for quite a while.

After Kee used the last piece of fry bread to wipe clean the bottom of the bowl and popped it in his mouth, he brought up the subject of the money that his boss wanted him to bring back. Seductively, she offered him personal favors until she received the money she was expecting at the end of the month. Kee found this temptation too great, and drove home feeling very guilty.

The guilt only added to the isolation in his soul. Now Annie was justified in her distance, even if she didn't know why. But Kee knew why and remembered that Pastor Bob had said sin separated us from God. He also had said that confessing our sins to God brought forgiveness. Kee tried this, but found it hard to forgive himself. How could he be forgiven after he had broken his lifetime promise to Annie? And what about Annie? Didn't she need to repent for something?

To make matters worse, when he visited the isolated hogan again at the end of the month the woman still didn't have money. This time it was easier to slip into the same ditch. Kee returned to Gallup and ended up giving some of his own cash to the boss on behalf of the woman. Though no one knew it was his, Kee felt even worse.

While at this spiritually low spot Kee went deeper into his dark cycle. It occurred to him that his pickup had much unused cargo space as he headed out to the reservation each day. Stopping to purchase some beer only seemed to make sense. Of course, it was not for him. No, he would never go back to drinking, but it was a way to get ahead financially.

When Annie found out about the beer running, her response was disastrous. She felt an instant suspicion of Kee. What else was he hiding? Was he going back to *all* his old ways? The unspoken questions turned into a thinly veiled resentment, and the resentment turned into rage and depression. With Carlita now in school, Annie had more freedom. She began hitching rides to Gallup and frequently bought her own beer before hitching a ride home.

Kee noticed the downward spiral in Annie and felt helpless to stop it. His own anger at her criticism and drunkenness made him want to withdraw into a shell of distant comfort, but where? The use of alcohol was a temptation that he could not resist forever, and he knew where that road would lead. A change was needed, and it came in the form of an invitation.

One day at the post office Kee received a flyer inviting him to a seminar on the book of Revelation at the theater in Window Rock. Fascination and hope sprang up within him as he looked at the flyer's strange pictures of the beasts in Revelation. He took it home to Annie.

"This is a study of the last book of the Bible," he began. "We should go. It could help us. We've not been following the road that made us happy."

Annie said nothing, but Kee made plans to attend. He missed the peace that he had known. It was the first pure joy he had known in his life. In anticipation of the refocusing, he stopped running beer out to the reservation.

On opening night he was there early. Annie had declined to come, yet he retained his hope. The theater filled up, and a young Navajo minister came out and spoke in a strong, friendly voice. He made the mysterious book seem simple. The discoveries were the positive spiritual distraction that Kee needed. He returned home with a glowing report for Annie.

The next night she and Carlita were sitting beside him. The child was a good reader and listened intently to the message. Afterward Willie, the minister, met them at the door and gave them a warm farewell.

Thus, another cycle began. The couple had their hearts warmed by the Word of God, and it followed that they warmed up to each other. As they studied the forgiveness of God, they forgave each other. The circle of love grew wider, and Carlita noticed the difference too.

One day Pastor Willie showed up at their door. Kee had mentioned where they lived, hoping he would come by, and it was a lift to see him standing outside. Inviting him in, Kee was pleased at his way of making them feel relaxed in his presence. After he visited for a while, he read them a promise from God's Holy Word and prayed for their home and individual lives. When he had finished, he stood to leave. Kee assured Pastor Willie that they would be at the meeting that night.

As each evening passed, Annie and Kee felt more complete in their understanding of the unconditional love of God. Pastor Willie showed not only the love but the way of staying in love with God and people. Kee was impressed that the pastor seemed to know more about the spiritual things than his dear, Anglo friend, Pastor Bob.

Toward the middle of the seminar this Navajo pastor revealed more of the forgotten mysteries of the Bible. The Sabbath, God's most intimate day with people, was news to Kee. It was amazing to learn that the Sabbath was actually on Saturday. That was the day that his people called "Little Sunday." They liked to go to town and shop on that day. He realized how out of harmony he was with the closeness that God was longing to share with him. This loving God won his heart, and the road of life was clearer than ever before.

After one of the meetings Kee spied an old, shirttail relative and crossed the crowded lobby to greet him. The old man was excited by what he was learning at the seminar too. After the customary greeting and handshake he went right into his latest discovery. "You know dis place in Mattyew 24:39 where it was da flood dat took da bad ones away? Dey use dat one to say its da rapchure—but it's da bad ones dat get taken away, like Pastor Willie says!"

Kee was familiar with the rapture theory from Pastor Bob. But he'd never thought to question his former spiritual leader until now. "Yes, and the part where Jesus said, 'In the world you *will have* tribulation!'" It made him wonder if the White man had only used the parts of the Holy Word that suited the beliefs that they already had. After all, hadn't they taken the Book from the Brown people in the east?

Pastor Willie showed how healthful living was taught in the Bible. This motivated Kee to eat more of the natural foods that his ancestors had used and to begin exercising in the early mornings again by running.

Soon the seminar was over, and Pastor Willie called for people to make a deeper decision about Jesus Christ and to renew themselves in baptism. Kee and Annie wanted this. They had finally found a love that was greater than their problems and their past. It was now or never for them, and they took their chance. Pastor Willie said he would meet them at Wheatfield Lake in the heart of Navajoland.

As they waded into the water, the slippery mud at the bottom seemed to make a final attempt to stop them, but they supported each other and reached the deeper area where the pastor was waiting for them. As they came up out of the water, they saw an eagle soaring in the mountains. It was a good sign that added confidence to their peace.

But baptism was only the beginning, and the many battles ahead lay hidden in the shadows beyond the light of those golden moments. Kee now understood the great controversy between good and evil in the world. He knew more about how to make a stand in the unseen spiritual war. He had more to learn about dealing with the people who attend a Christian church and still travel between the edges of light and darkness.

CHAPTER 12

The Cost of Greatness

"There is a way which seemeth right unto a man" (Proverbs 14:12).

KEE AWOKE WITH HIS heart pounding. He blinked rapidly, trying to get his eyes to focus. The darkness told him that it was still deep in the night. Feeling the bed covers and hearing Annie's soft breathing next to him brought the realization of where he was. But it comforted him little. His ears strained to hear any other sound, as he recalled the upsetting dream.

He remembered that he had been walking on the side of the highway between Window Rock and Gallup when he had heard a great roaring behind him. Turning, he saw a towering wall of water, at least 200 feet high, coming straight toward him between the gap in the mesas. In desperation he ran down the road, then realized that it would catch him unless he could run up the side of one of the mesas. He sprinted with all his might up the brushy slope, but he could see the wall of water gaining on him. As the spray from the lead wave began to hit him, he left the dream and regained consciousness.

Deeply disturbed by the dream, Kee lay awake, thinking and praying. The way of his people was to take dreams seriously. He would tell Annie in the morning; you always should tell your bad dreams to someone so that they are less likely to happen. But in the meantime, Kee earnestly asked God not to let the dream actually happen to him. He was sure it was a sign to get out of this area of Navajoland.

The invisible things of life affect the visible, and the opposite is also true. Annie and Kee were happy again. The painful past was behind them, and yet there were still things of a basic nature that were unresolved. For Kee the issue of having a job that didn't pull him back into the old life was important. Besides, he was tired of the long days of driving away from the family and the hassle of prying money out of people. He needed a healthier occupation. Annie, on the other hand, needed more fulfillment in her life now that Carlita was out of the house more and enjoying her own circle of friends. She also needed to work closer with Kee and guard their reestablished intimacy. She hadn't been able to bond with a Christian woman because unlike Pastor Bob, young Pastor Willie had no wife to whom she could open up. Even so, she had come along with Kee through the process and was giving it her all.

Kee didn't share Annie's lack of bonding. He was very comfortable with Pastor Willie and shared with him his desire to get into a different occupation. Every day he worked for the furniture store grated on his nerves a little more. He explained to the pastor some of his background and difficulty with this job, without a direct reference to the bootlegging and loose living. He then asked a life-altering question.

"Pastor, is there anywhere that you can think of where Annie and I might be able to work together for the Lord?"

Pastor Willie didn't rush his answer. He knew that Kee and Annie were new Christians, and he didn't want to set them up for failure. Yet it was obvious that Kee's abilities and talents were needed in many places. He wished he could keep them right near him for a while. He could train them in ministry and build up the local church as well. "Let me think about it" was all he would say.

A couple weeks later he came by the little house and visited Kee and Annie for some time before bringing up the real purpose for his visit. "There's a Christian Indian school that needs some help," he began. "It's off the reservation, but many of our Navajo children go there. Maybe you should think about giving them a call and going over to check it out—they may be looking for Christian Navajos to take some of the jobs."

Kee and Annie were very interested and asked a lot of questions about the school. Pastor Willie did his best to answer them, but the truth was he didn't know much about this institution. Before he left he gave them the school's number.

The couple talked about it long after Pastor Willie was down the road. It sounded very interesting to them. They had never been able to work in a Christian setting before and thought it would be wonderful to have such an environment for work.

Kee called the school the very next day to arrange a time to visit with the head administrator. The Anglo man sounded very positive. He wanted Kee and Annie to come over as soon as possible for an interview.

The school was a considerable distance from the little house, so Kee and Annie had to hitch a ride to reach the location. When they saw the campus they were impressed. Never had a government school looked this nice! There was a church, nice dormitories for the older children, and group houses for the youngest children. Kee found himself remembering his educational experience and wishing that he had been able to live in such a place.

The visit with the school administrator was pleasant enough. He asked questions about their experience and education. He genuinely wanted to hire more Native workers for this school. Kee knew that many of these institutions wanted people with a college education, and this made him worry about their chances. At the end of the visit the school leader asked to have their telephone number so he could call them if anything opened up. Kee gave Pastor Willie's number since they didn't have one of their own.

Kee and Annie hitched a ride home and prayed each morning and evening that they'd get the job. A week later, while attending a prayer meeting, they noticed Pastor Willie's smile as he told them of a phone call he'd received from the school that day. He said there were jobs for both of them!

They asked for more details, but Pastor Willie had no more information. They must call the school and find out. The couple could hardly sleep that night. There was a lightness in their hearts and an excitement that was clean and good.

When morning finally arrived, they called. The administrator said they needed a man who would keep the school grounds nice, and a woman who would help teach Native art and also back up the girls' dean. He went on to say that they had a rent-free house for them, and stipends totaling $2,000 a month.

Kee and Annie were delighted. At last they could reach their dreams together! It was so hard to succeed at leaving the reservation lifestyle, but now they could do it in an honorable way. Joyfully Annie began packing. She would let her younger sisters use the little house while they were gone. This way, she would be able to help them out while she went into a better situation herself. Carlita, a young teenager by now, was not thrilled about moving away from her friends, but this new school did sound interesting.

On the arranged day a pickup from the school arrived, and the family and their possessions were loaded up and taken to the Christian Indian school. For the first time, Kee felt really good about going to school!

Moving in took longer than the truck ride, and Kee, true to his roots, went to the administrator to ask for a cash advance to help him get some things they needed for their new place. The money was given, and Kee went out and bought some furniture that he knew Annie had wanted for some time. A friendly staff member gave him a ride and helped him cart the furniture back to the campus.

The children would be arriving in a few days for another year of education. So the staff was brought together for numerous meetings in the hopes of building unity and purpose among the workers. Kee found these gatherings very stimulating and enjoyed them immensely. Unlike Kee, Annie felt overwhelmed by the large gatherings of people from different cultures. Nevertheless, she found many people in the group who were very friendly to her. The only exception was a staff member from some county far to the east. This woman seemed to avoid her and would never shake her hand.

When she told Kee about it one evening, he was surprised. What did this mean? Wasn't everyone a Christian here? Puzzled, he tried to give the staff member the benefit of the doubt.

"Maybe she's just having a bad day," he suggested.

"Den it's been a bad two days!" Annie retorted.

"Well, maybe she's slipped away from the Lord," he replied. "You know it happened like that to us."

Once the children arrived, the couple was immersed in a whirlwind of activities. Kee was busy not only with the grounds, but also with driving sick children to the clinic, helping move equipment, and even giving an occasional worship talk to the children. They seemed to gravitate toward him, and he loved the chance to give them something that he never had the chance to receive during his own childhood.

Annie was busy setting up a pottery program for the children and teaching weaving to some of the older girls on the side. She was happy when one of the administrators said that the children could sell their creations and make some profit. She told the good news to her classes, and they got excited too. Her relief work at the girls' dorm was also positive. The head dean noticed that her bold correction of the children's misbehavior produced immediate results. The girls regarded her with the same level of respect one of their own relatives would command.

A wonderful year flew by, interspersed with only minor flareups when the woman from the eastern county would give Annie the cold shoulder. At those times she usually came home and dumped the details and her emotion on Kee. He tried to calm her with his gentle comments, and this seemed to work well enough.

Carlita became heavily involved in the school's traveling choir and, more importantly, was becoming very involved in the spiritual activities of the school. Her boldness for Christ led her to speak to many of her schoolmates about the love and power of God in her life. She knew that many of them came from the same insanity in which she had grown up throughout her childhood. However, they didn't have parents who were making changes for the better; they were feeling alone in the world—lonely for love and often depressed.

When the week of prayer arrived, Carlita was asked to give her testimony. It was hard to stand in front of her fellow students, and harder still to share about her not-so-distant childhood pain. But she did, and it made a major impact on her classmates. Ten of them, including Carlita, joined the baptismal class.

Before the summer vacation arrived, Carlita and seven others, wearing robes, stood in line next to the baptistry in the campus church. Some of the younger children smiled in their embarrassment, but the older ones looked on with mixed emotions. Some were envious of their courage but fearful to follow their example, and somewhat doubtful of the benefits of such a step. Carlita, however, was not at all concerned about their thoughts. She was doing this for Jesus and the truth. It was the happiest day of her life!

As she went down into the water, she saw a light and a beautiful rainbow surrounding her. No one else noticed, not even Kee and Annie, who sat in the congregation with tears running down their bronze cheeks. It was all wonderful enough for them.

As the summer began, they planned to return to the little house. The administrator said that he would travel with the pottery the students had made during the year and sell it at different meetings. Then, when the children returned, they would receive the benefit from the sales. Annie was satisfied with this and informed her classes of the plan.

Kee didn't have to borrow anyone's vehicle anymore. He was driving his own pickup and was very pleased with it. He loaded their belongings up, and they headed back to the Window Rock area—without Carlita. She had been asked to travel with some of the staff during the summer to help sell artwork and promote the school. There would be times when she would come home between events. This was important to her—she wanted to share her new faith with her old friends at the public school.

On her first break she went door to door with her Bible, sharing her new experience. Many of the teens were impressed, and a few even came to Pastor Willie's church services. But it was hard to compete with the lights, glitter, and entertainment of the television. Most of Carlita's old friends were already steeped in the music and culture of Hollywood. When she was gone on tour for the school, her friends quit coming to church. After a two-week absence, she returned to find that her friends were no longer interested. The road seemed too hard to follow. It was a road that went against the current of their peers, and Carlita wasn't there regularly enough to help them with the change. Disappointed, she attended Pastor Willie's church without them. True, her parents were there, but she missed her own age group and wanted to share her inner peace with them.

At the end of summer the family moved back to their house at the school. Each of them was excited about the coming school year. It was to be Carlita's junior year, Annie had new ideas for her art classes, and Kee was thinking about how he might be of more help to the troubled students. He remembered his teacher, Mr. Martinez, in Phoenix, and how he had helped him years ago. He wanted to make a difference in the lives of the children.

However, this year would make an even bigger difference in their own lives, testing them severely. The trials began at the staff meetings, before the children arrived. The same woman from the east had returned and was now in charge of the supplies. Now Kee noticed her attitude as well when she refused to shake his hand. Shaking hands was common courtesy among his people. He left the gathering with a bad feeling in his heart. What was this woman doing here? Would she treat the children the same way? When Annie expressed her feelings about the woman, Kee could no longer give her the benefit of the doubt. He only affirmed her feeling with his comment, "I hope she doesn't do it to the kids. We need to pray for her."

Prayer works, but it doesn't always work in the manner, and with the speed, we desire. Kee began watching the woman and noticed her manner with other people. It was clear that she classified people and treated them differently. Another Navajo couple on campus was getting the same treatment she gave Kee and Annie. Whenever they tried to get quilts or food that had been donated for the children and workers, this woman would refuse them, or only give them the bare minimum. Kee noticed other Anglo staff members receiving more items whenever they went to her. Further, he noticed that the quilts she gave to the dormitory children were the worn ones, while other staff received the more beautifully worked comforters.

And Annie was having new troubles of her own. One day a child came into her classroom crying, saying that the business office was not giving her any money for the artwork she had made during the previous school year. Annie knew that this girl's creations had been sold during the summer, so she indignantly made her way to the office to straighten the matter out immediately.

"What is going on around here?" she began. "Why didn't Lucinda get her money?"

"Well, Annie," said the administrator, "she did get money. Didn't we tell you how it was going to work? It was credited to her school bill, and that's why she was able to come back this year."

"What about da utter part?" Annie asked with suspicion.

"We charged each child 20 percent for the school's cost of taking the art work around and selling it. So that part of the sale went directly to the school on a consignment basis."

"Dat's not what you told me last year!" she stormed. "You told me dat da kids would be getting money for der work, an dat's what I told dem!"

The administrator's face flushed. "Annie, I'm sorry if there has been a

118

misunderstanding, but you know how important it is for these students to help with their school bill. Perhaps we can arrange to give them a small percentage of spending money too. Let me meet with our principal and see what he says, and then I will let you know."

"You made me a liar to deez kids," she said with firmness. "You are using dem for your own things! Carlita went with you all summer, and she's da one who sat at da table selling dat art, not da school. So you charged her too, huh? I don't trust you anymore!"

With that she walked out, leaving a shaken man in the business office. It was an unfortunate incident that no amount of reasoning with her would mend. Shortly after this visit, adjustments were made to give each child some pocket money for their art work. But it didn't change the shadow of suspicion in Annie's heart.

Carlita heard the rumblings at home about these things, and it troubled her too. She wondered how Christians could do these kinds of things to other people. She was not able to objectively look at the situation from both sides. Nor could her parents. To make matters worse, they heard that Pastor Willie was leaving the area. So their support at the home church in Window Rock was diminished. The family went back to the little house on one of their weekends off and managed to visit Pastor Willie on his last Sabbath at church.

"Don't worry; the Lord only wants you to do your part," he encouraged. "Don't let other people stop you from doing the right thing. This world will be over soon, and God will deal with the people who did badly to you!" He went on to tell them about another good pastor who was coming to take his place. "He's really good with our people," he promised. "I've known him for a long time."

Kee struggled inwardly with yet another abandonment by a pastor, but outwardly he simply asked, "Is he not Diné [one of our people]?"

"No, but he's not like most other Bilagaanas [Anglos]," Pastor Willie replied. "Just give him a chance, and you will see!"

Sadly they said farewell to Pastor Willie. He had been used by God to turn their lives around. What would they do without him? Would this experience be a repeat of losing Pastor Bob?

They didn't have to wait long to find out. The new pastor was very different. For one thing, he knew the Navajo hymns better than most of the local congregation. He always greeted them and said blessings to them in their own language. The longer he stayed on the reservation, the longer his hair grew, until he occasionally wore the traditional bun behind his neck. When asked about why he had long hair, his answer was simple and amusing. "To the Navajos, long hair is a sign of wisdom," he would say. "So I'm trying to get some wisdom!"

At first Kee was cautious. This man was strange to him, and both he and Annie had put more distance between themselves and Anglos. Anglos always left or let you down, so why get too close? But Kee knew in his heart that this man truly cared about him and his family. He talked about his desire for Kee to come and help him work for the Lord on the reservation. As things became increasingly difficult at the school, Kee liked this idea more and more. Whenever there was a free Sabbath, he returned to the Window Rock church group to visit with his Christian family there. He had become disillusioned with the school's issues over intricacies that didn't make sense to him. "Who cares what the accreditation committee or OSHA thinks?" he wondered. "And why do some of these volunteers act so grumpy? Aren't they glad to be serving the Lord?"

Each time he returned from a visit home the desire within him grew to make a change. Early in the spring the new pastor offered Kee a job as a Bible worker, and Kee accepted. He liked the idea of working among his people on the reservation, fulfilling his dream of ministry. He thought he was strong enough to resist the temptations that would inevitably be waiting for him there.

Annie was just as distant as he from her original joy of being at the school. However, she knew there was no work for her on the reservation. She decided to stay on at the school where she enjoyed her art work and found fulfillment in helping the children. Her duties were lighter on weekends, so she could join her family at the little house during those breaks.

The most painful change, though, was what was happening inside Carlita. Her misunderstanding had turned to resentment, and the resentment to bitterness. She no longer wanted to be at school or attend church, despite her parents' encouragement. Kee was worried about his daughter, and thought that if she came home with him it might help her attitude.

Kee dove into his work. The new pastor encouraged him to become a self-educated success. "You don't need a college degree," he assured Kee. "Just be a man of the Word, and God will make you a success!" He involved Kee in many parts of reservation ministry that were beyond the scope of a Bible worker. They operated a food pantry for the needy, provided transportation, and worked on repair projects.

One day the new pastor came to Kee about a problem that Kee had assumed was a private family matter. "Kee," he began, "have you read what it says in the book of Timothy on the requirements for an elder?"

Kee had not, so the pastor read it to him, emphasizing the part that talks about managing your own family and children. "Kee," he continued, "I was out at your house when your daughter was drunk and tearing things up. When I tried to talk to her, she said that her boyfriend has been sleeping over there, too. People in the community are starting to talk about your home and its troubles, and I don't want them to lose their respect for you, Kee. What if you were to move out of the little house and live in the church? That way, nobody can blame you for what is happening at the house. It's either that, or you must tell Carlita to leave the house if she wants to continue living this way. If you don't take a stand against this, Kee, it will be the same as supporting the thing that is killing her, and your own people will not listen to your sermons."

Grieved, Kee said he would think about it. He knew that his daughter was heavily into alcohol. He had even found cans of hair spray in the yard and feared that she was mixing the can's contents with water and making the toxic drink called "ocean." Clearly, something had to be done, but he didn't like this pastor's way of meddling. When he told Annie about it, her reaction was even more potent.

"What is dat man trying to do to us?" she sobbed. "Is he trying to tear our home apart until none of us are together?"

"I think he's trying to help," said Kee, "but how can I kick my daughter out, like my mother did to me? Carlita's going to have a baby soon—we will lose our grandchild if she leaves."

"He is trying to ruin our family!" Annie countered. "Why don't you come back to da Indian school and work with me?"

Kee paused. He knew that Carlita would not return to the school with them. However, if he left, the little house would be hers, and the little grandchild would be theirs. "I think I will call that administrator tomorrow," he said with new resolve.

When the telephone rang in the school's main office, the timing couldn't have been better. The school had just lost a couple disgruntled staff members, and Kee could definitely help fill the gap in the program. As he moved back to the school, he felt grateful that things were still working his way. However, Kee's biggest trial lay just ahead, and he had no idea how hard it would hit him.

On the way to the school, Annie told him that the woman from the eastern county was gone now. Kee felt relief not only for the children, but for himself. That was the secret—if he just could stay around long enough all the problematic people would go away!

Kee's work at the school was more diversified than before. He transported children, covered as a dean, counseled children, and served as a night watchman. He was intelligent enough to understand that a number of workers were getting paid more for doing the same work that he was doing simply because they had a higher education degree. It was a system that he thought was unfair. As the weeks passed, he did everything he was asked, but inwardly he was grieved by the situation and missed the work that he had left behind in Window Rock.

He also worried about his daughter. On his trips home he tried to encourage her, but it was obvious that her problem with alcohol was only getting worse. He told her to contact the new pastor, and at her times of lowest despair she did. The long-haired pastor and his wife would come over and pray with her.

Then the unexpected blow fell. The administrator called Kee and Annie to the office and told them of reports he was getting from the reservation about Kee selling drugs and Annie using drugs. He simply asked if these reports were true.

Kee was stunned beyond words. In his mind he went back to the bad medicine that some people used against others in order to make them turn against their own kind. He wondered if this was what was happening to his family. Annie found her tongue much more quickly, and her anger was enough to intimidate anyone.

"Should I ask you if all da stuff we hear about you is true?" she fumed. "What if we did dat? People just want to hurt us, but da Lord knows us! He doesn't care what anybody else says about us!"

The administrator apologized and explained that he had a responsibility to check on anything that was said about the staff. He closed with a prayer that seemed inadequate to change the mood in the room.

Kee and Annie left the office feeling wounded. Who would say such things about them? Why would anyone want to destroy their lives?

As the weeks passed, the administrator received more phone calls from people who reported seeing Kee and Annie selling and using drugs on the reservation. Again he called the couple in, with the same results. But this time when Kee and Annie left, it was with the bitterness that comes when you finally lose all your drive to fulfill a higher cause.

At the end of the school year the couple moved to another location. The administrator had decided not to renew their contract for the coming year, but it didn't matter. They didn't want to continue their work at the school. Kee had decided to go to college. Even though he was now a grandpa, he wanted to reach a higher level of understanding and status. Annie was interested in her new grandson, and worked at a grocery store.

The blur of difficulty went on, and Kee's desire for an education seemed more out of reach as the practical realities forced themselves upon him. It was hard to pay the rent, provide for the family needs, and still get a decent grade. He quit school and managed to get a position as a janitor at a public school.

One day while Annie was staying with Carlita and the baby, Kee went back to his old home on the mesa. The desire to help his people came back to him as he looked over the edge at the old sheep camp. Grandpa and Grandma were gone now, and their hogan was partially torn down. They had died not knowing the truth that he knew. Tears welled up in his eyes as he tried to picture them doing their chores in the encampment below. He had wasted so many chances; he must start again to help his people find the beautiful road.

Hiking down the mesa, he hurried to his pickup. Soon a cloud of dust was all that remained of him, and like the phantom of his ancestors, it too was soon gone. The road led him back to the Window Rock church and the long-haired pastor's home where, after several minutes of friendly conversation, he disclosed the real purpose of his visit.

"I was wondering if you needed a good Navajo Bible worker."

The pastor caught his meaning immediately and replied, "Well, I always need some good help like you, but I have no more money." He went on to explain that he had already hired a replacement, and until he raised more funds he could not pay Kee for his help.

"I wish our church supported the unreached peoples of North America the way they do the foreign missions," the pastor went on. "Then there would be money for you. But I *do* need your help—there are still 200,000 of your people to reach!"

Kee understood the money problem. He also comprehended the complications of having his large reservation divided into so many separate church conferences and unions that divided the Navajo work. But he also knew Annie was counting on him to support her and Carlita. He could see no way to do the work he had hoped to do. So on he drove to a coal mine where he applied for work and was hired. The pay at the mine was the best he had ever received, and he now found himself supporting his aging mother and younger brother's family, as well as his own family.

Kee never forgot his dream of sharing the Good News. He began to share his faith on the job until his supervisor told him to quit preaching or be fired.

In time the new pastor moved away, and Pastor Willie returned. Kee was happy to see him again, though it flew in the face of his inner expectation that everyone important to him would abandon him, sooner or later. He realized that the bitterness in his soul was a part of the same evil he had despised in others. It was a problem to overcome. He began to attend the Navajo church again with Annie. Kee enjoyed Anglos, but he knew that Annie felt more comfortable with her own people. Another problem was developing, though, and unlike some of the others, this attack came from within Kee's physical body.

Early one morning he was awakened by a terrible pain in his side. Annie was still sleeping, but he couldn't wait. He shook her gently until she stirred. "I have terrible pain right here," he said, pointing to his abdomen.

"Should I get a medicine root for you and make tea?"

"No; take me to a hospital. I'm not sure if I'll make it if I wait for the tea!"

The hospital emergency room was crowded, but the secretary realized that Kee's condition was serious and rushed him into an examining room. Soon he was being attended by a doctor, an IV was inserted, and blood was drawn for tests. Annie's frightened eyes were still beautiful as she helplessly watched over Kee. He had always insulated her from the harshest parts of life. Now he was fading in and out of consciousness.

The lab report was not favorable. Kee's liver was not functioning properly. If things didn't change, he would be gone soon. In desperation, Annie rushed to a pay phone and called a church member in Window Rock. The member assured her that the church would be alerted and begin praying right away.

Hours, and then days, passed. In his unconscious state, Kee felt himself moving into a dream. He saw a bright light approaching him, swelling until it penetrated his skin. When it reached his painful spot, it turned into a warm feeling that brought relief. The warm sensation continued until it woke him. The overhead light was the first thing he saw. Annie sat wearily in a chair next to him, a magazine from the hospital lobby lay unheeded in her lap. She heard him stir and looked up, surprised.

"You OK?"

"Yes, but I'm thirsty!"

"Kee, da church has been praying for you," she tearfully confessed, "and da Lord helped you fight dis one!"

A wave of feelings and wordless pictures flooded into his consciousness. Scenes of the love and goodness that had managed to reach him throughout his painful journey suddenly returned for his review. Gratitude swelled until it washed the sides of the dry canyon in his soul. Tears welled up, but never quite reached his cheeks.

"Yes," Kee replied, "He is very good!"

Annie got him water from the pitcher beside his bed. Kee's eyes glanced around the room until they reached the window. He could see that he was facing the west side of Gallup. The distant hills and mesas were a visual comfort to him. Above the far-off Chushka Mountains an eagle circled. A small ember of hope within his soul flared anew into a flame. The eternal plan would never be completely lost.

He took a sip of water and thought about what he would like to do when he got out of the hospital. There was little that appealed to him anymore. But the dream of helping his own people as a Bible worker filled his mind again. Maybe the Lord had saved him from death for the purpose of service. No matter what would unfold for him, Kee knew that he was loved with an everlasting love. Others may not be so quick to forget their old memories of him, but he was free. His simplicity clung to him. He was thankful for what he had learned from his victories—and his defeats.

His unfinished life was somehow bound with the life of his people. Together, his life and the life of his people, were like the rock formations of the sun-baked southwest—beaten by the winds of change, eroded by the rains of many storms, yet intact and barely penetrated.

The final chapters of this story are yet to be written because Kee still lives, breathes, and searches for a way. But one can be certain that he is somewhere watching the unseen reminders of his Creator, and standing courageously against the darkness that always stalks him.

In his solitary struggles he will ever be the Spirit Warrior.

YOU can make a difference!

Service Opportunities at Native Ministry Outposts

There are many opportunities for caring people to make a short- or long-term commitment to serve in one of the many neglected Native communities in the United States and Canada. For more information about specifics, contact:

Monte Church
North Pacific Union Conference of Seventh-day Adventists
P.O. Box 16670
Portland, OR 97292-0670

If you would like to join the author in an adventure in his present field of service, you may contact David George by e-mail: loneassyrian@hotmail.com.

Mission Trips to Native Ministry Outposts:

Any of the locations listed below would welcome a person or team coming to help with a service project or ministry effort. In most of these locations it is also a struggle to find adequate financial resources to serve Native people.

Arizona:
Chinle Seventh-day Adventist Church
P.O. Box 2299
Chinle, Arizona 86503
520-674-5692

Holbrook Adventist Indian School
P.O. Box 880
Holbrook, Arizona 86025
928-524-6845

Maricopa Seventh-day Adventist
  Church
Route 1, Box 195
Laveen, Arizona 85339

Window Rock Seventh-day Adventist
  Church
Window Rock, Arizona 86515

Canada:
Mamawi Atosketan Native School
Rural Route 2
Ponoka, Alberta, Canada T4J 1R2

Maskwachees Seventh-day Adventist
  Company
Box 788
Hobbema, Alberta, Canada T0C 1N0

Montana:
Fort Peck Church Group
Montana Conference of Seventh-day
  Adventists
175 Canyon View Road
Bozeman, Montana 59715
406-587-3101

Fort Belknap Church Group
Pastor, Seventh-day Adventist Church
405 Sixth Street
Havre, Montana, 59501
406-265-4601

New Mexico:
La Vida Mission
P.O. Box 3308
Farmington, New Mexico 87499

Utah:
Monument Valley Seventh-day
  Adventist Church
7 Rock Door Canyon
P.O. Box 360015
Monument Valley, Utah 84536
435-727-3239